FORWARD PASS

"It seems that Coach Gardner is desperate for a decent pass catcher for his Aldridge High Panthers. Otherwise, he must muddle through a dismal season with a ground game alone. Jill Winston is the surprise he comes up with—an athletic girl who has already shown that she can catch a ball from her basketball experience. . . . Dygard takes readers carefully and convincingly through the maze of problems that the coach must maneuver to get his new star onto the field. . . . Somehow, he makes it all sound believable, and there's the extra fillip of good description of football action."

—*School Library Journal*

PUFFIN BOOKS BY THOMAS J. DYGARD

The Rookie Arrives
Tournament Upstart
Halfback Tough
Quarterback Walk-On
Winning Kicker
Soccer Duel
Forward Pass

FORWARD PASS

THOMAS J. DYGARD

PUFFIN BOOKS

PUFFIN BOOKS
Published by the Penguin Group
Viking Penguin, a division of Penguin Books USA Inc.,
375 Hudson Street, New York, New York 10014, U.S.A.
Penguin Books Ltd, 27 Wrights Lane, London W8 5TZ, England
Penguin Books Australia Ltd, Ringwood, Victoria, Australia
Penguin Books Canada Ltd, 10 Alcorn Avenue, Toronto, Ontario, Canada M4V 3B2
Penguin Books (N.Z.) Ltd, 182–190 Wairau Road, Auckland 10, New Zealand

Penguin Books Ltd, Registered Offices: Harmondsworth, Middlesex, England

First published in the United States of America
by William Morrow and Company, Inc., 1989
Reprinted by arrangement with William Morrow and Company, Inc.
Published in Puffin Books 1990
5 7 9 10 8 6 4

LIBRARY OF CONGRESS CATALOGING IN PUBLICATION DATA
Dygard, Thomas J.   Forward Pass / by Thomas J. Dygard.   p. cm.
Summary: To improve his struggling football team's chances of
winning, Coach Gardner brings in a new wide receiver, Jill Winston.
ISBN 0-14-034562-0
[1. Football—Fiction.   2. Sex role—Fiction.   3. High schools—
Fiction.   4. Schools—Fiction.]   I. Title.
[PZ7.D9893Fo 1990]   [Fic]—dc20   90-8459

Printed in the United States of America
Set in Primer

FOR
RAAF STEVENS

CHAPTER

Frank Gardner, heading into his second year as football coach of the Aldridge High Panthers, sat at the desk in his small office off the gymnasium and drummed his fingers nervously, awaiting the arrival of Jill Winston.

The bell signaling the beginning of the third period—a study hall for Jill—had just rung, and she would be along shortly, undoubtedly puzzled by a summons from the football coach.

Frank turned in his chair and looked out the window toward the football practice field, the grass a dull brownish color with the last days of summer turning into the first days of autumn. His mind went forward to the fast-approaching football season. The first game was less than two weeks away. Following the first game were nine straight Friday nights of games, leading to the championship of the North-Central Conference for one of the teams—but probably not the Aldridge High Panthers.

The coming season looked as though it would be a rerun of the previous one—lucky to break even, to win five of the games.

Frank Gardner's first Aldridge High team had a decent-enough running game, quick, with strong ball carriers operating behind a strong line. And the Panthers had an outstanding quarterback in Scott Butler, an excellent ball handler and an able passer. All of those good ingredients were returning for their senior year in Frank Gardner's second season at the helm.

But there was one hitch: There was no one to catch Scott Butler's bullet passes.

There were pass receivers, sure—Eddie McMahon at end, Lenny Parker at wide receiver—but neither they nor anyone else on the team possessed the natural talent, the exceptional hands, the something extra that completed a consistently dangerous passing attack.

So the Panthers had no effective passing strategy to go with their strong running game.

Opposing teams, aware of the fact that the Panthers posed no serious threat in the air, zeroed in on the running attack, recklessly blitzing, always charging. They nailed the runners in their tracks.

Yes, the Aldridge High Panthers had been lucky to win five of their games in Frank Gardner's first season.

Frank had learned quickly upon arriving at Aldridge High that the North-Central Conference, while comprised of small high schools, was the center of a hotbed of football in northern Illinois. At all of the schools, the major athletic emphasis was on football. The top athletes played football first, then maybe another sport—but always football first. The conference, from top to bottom, consisted of tough teams.

And by season's end Frank had learned that around the town of Aldridge—on the streets, in the cafes, in the corridors of the school—five victories was considered far short of a satisfactory total. Very far short.

The Aldridge High Panthers had a history of winning seasons, but they had not won a North-Central Conference championship in almost a dozen years. With their winning seasons they had come close to capturing the crown several times. But coming close was not a championship. The Aldridge High fans were hungry for a championship trophy.

Finally the pressure from the fans had sent the previous coach packing for another job, leading to Frank's hiring. Frank had won two championships at a small school in southern Indiana. He was a championship coach. He was going to bring the trophy home to Aldridge.

But Frank's first-season record of five victories, three of them in the conference, was a long way from a championship.

Now his second season loomed. And unless a miracle occurred, the Panthers were going to need a lot of luck to even match the previous season's record.

The spring drills, despite all the combinations Frank tried, turned up nobody able to hang on to Scott Butler's bullet passes with consistency.

But long before the spring drills, Frank Gardner had had an idea, a crazy idea, the kind of idea that miracles—and disasters, too—are made of.

He knew almost the precise moment that the idea came into his head. It was February 14—Valentine's Day—and the time was a few minutes after eight o'clock in the evening. Frank was sitting with his wife, Carol, in the bleachers of the Aldridge High gymnasium. They were in the crowd watching the Aldridge High girls' basketball team play the Ashville Bears.

There was a wild scramble for a loose ball under the Aldridge High basket. Everyone was reaching and clawing and diving for it. One of the Aldridge High players finally got the ball, took a firm grip with both hands, and pivoted away from the crowd.

Another Aldridge High player, seeing that her teammate had the ball, broke into a run down the court, looking back for a pass. She was tall, probably close to six feet, muscular but in a sleek, slender way. She was not brawny. She ran easily, with the loping cadence of a natural athlete.

Frank Gardner knew her name: Jill Winston.

The player with the ball under the basket fired a long, two-handed pass down the court, out in front of the racing Jill Winston. The pass looked at first to have too much lead on it. Surely it was going beyond Jill's reach. The ball would bounce out of bounds at the other end of the court, a scoring opportunity lost.

Jill shifted a gear somewhere inside her body. Her

speed increased. She reached up with her right hand, eyes on the ball.

But the ball was going beyond her.

Too bad. Frank Gardner knew that in basketball as well as in football, an inch here and an inch there—a puny little inch—could make the difference between victory and defeat.

Then Jill leaped, a smooth and graceful springing motion without breaking stride. Her right hand, outstretched, reached for the ball. She got a finger, then another, in contact with it. The ball seemed to respond to her touch, to decide on its own that such an outstanding effort deserved a reward. The ball succumbed to Jill's control. Jill brought it in easily, dribbled twice, went up, and laid the ball in the basket for a field goal.

The Aldridge High fans leaped to their feet all around the gymnasium and roared their approval.

Frank leaped to his feet with them. But he was not roaring his approval. He stood up so he could see the finish of the play, but he was frowning in thought. Beside him Carol was smiling and clapping her hands. But Frank did not cheer. He watched and weighed the idea that was forming in his mind.

The vision of the rangy girl with the fluid movements coaxing the ball into her hands stayed with Frank Gardner through the evening, and then through the weeks leading up to spring football practice, and then through the long months of summer, until the day of football sign-up a week ago.

□ 5 □

More than once Frank tried to shrug off the idea. It was too crazy. But the idea stayed with him.

At one point he tried a variation on the idea. If a girl basketball player put visions of a superb pass receiver in his mind, why not a boy basketball player? The receiver he needed—with perfect coordination, good hands— might be on the boys' basketball team.

But several of the boys on the basketball team already were on the football team. They were football players enjoying a second sport in the off-season. They finished the football season and then joined the basketball team a few weeks after the start of practice. The other basketball players, Frank found, were either pint-sized little sharpshooters, not pass receivers, or gangly boys who offered height in place of talent. Nothing there.

Frank went back to thinking about Jill Winston—the rangy girl who raced downcourt with surprising speed and pulled in a pass she had, by all rights, no hope of catching. And this time he did more than reflect on the picture of Jill Winston in action. He set out to find out who she was.

She was uniform number 6 on the Aldridge High girls' basketball team. She was the best player on the team. She was, according to the game program, a junior who stood five feet, ten inches tall and weighed one hundred thirty-two pounds. She was a face he had seen in the corridors in his first year at Aldridge High. Sometimes she was walking with Henry Allison, a tackle on the football team. But what else?

Frank found out easily enough that Jill was the daughter of Mr. and Mrs. Palmer Winston. That might be good news, Frank figured. Palmer Winston's photograph hung in the gymnasium lobby. Now a prominent Aldridge attorney, he had captained the Panthers' football team almost thirty years earlier. His son had played for the Panthers six years ago. So Jill was the daughter and younger sister of athletes. Small wonder that she had the physique, coordination, and competitive spirit necessary for athletic success. More important, from Frank's standpoint, was the fact that Palmer Winston had been a football player, and his son had been a football player. Why not his daughter? Palmer Winston might—just might—buy the idea.

That is, if Jill herself bought the idea. Would Jill want to play football? She might simply laugh and say no. But, Frank told himself, Jill was an athlete—girl or boy—and she might respond to the challenge.

Through it all, a troublesome question kept recurring in Frank's mind: Could he guarantee her safety?

Jill herself probably would ask it. Certainly her parents would ask it. Frank would have to give them an answer that satisfied. He also, doubtless, would have to provide an answer to the question from others—school officials, conference officials, the townspeople of Aldridge, even perhaps his own players.

At one hundred thirty-two pounds, Jill weighed as much as some of the boys—Eddie McMahon, for one—who were playing on the team. But that was not a satisfying answer.

There were ways to minimize the dangers. But to *elim-*

inate them? Frank knew it was impossible. Jill would know it, too, and so would her father.

There was another question, too: a *girl* catching Scott Butler's bullet passes? Frank smiled at the question.

The summer passed as Frank toyed with the idea, juggling his answers to the questions that kept popping up in his mind.

Then it was Monday of the third week of August.

The day of football sign-up was the last chance for a miracle to occur—a miracle in the form of a transfer student, newly moved to Aldridge with his family, offering superb pass-catching skills to the Panthers.

But as Frank watched the boys signing up at the table in the gymnasium—most of them familiar faces—and later as he scanned the list of names, he knew that no miracle had occurred delivering into his fold a top-caliber pass receiver for the Panthers.

Again the picture of the girl going up for the ball, touching it, bringing it in, returned to his mind, and Frank decided he was going to have to produce the miracle himself.

That was when he first put the idea into words, asking his assistant, Ron Matthews, new on the job with a degree from Indiana University, what he thought.

Ron responded with silence, widening eyes, and a dropping jaw. Then he said, "A girl?"

"You haven't seen her," Frank said. "She's a tremendous athlete."

"But . . . a girl?"

Frank decided to back off to give Ron time to let the idea jell. "It's just an idea," he said. "Think about it. But keep it to yourself, okay? I haven't discussed this with anyone else."

But Frank knew what he was going to do.

Now, for more than a week, he had pondered the proper course to take. He considered beginning with Elaine Carter, the girls' basketball coach. It would be, first of all, a matter of courtesy. The football coach seeking a share of the girls' basketball coach's talented player should of course touch base with the girls' basketball coach. Elaine Carter was always talking about equal opportunities for girls, so she should be supportive of a revolutionary plan offering an unusual opportunity to a girl.

But no, Frank had seen and heard enough of Elaine Carter in faculty meetings and in day-to-day contact to know her immediate reaction: No way. She viewed her basketball players as her personal property. She took care of them, stood up for them, fought for them—and they won for her. She was not about to let go of one of them for another sport without a fight. Besides, the end of the football season overlapped with the beginning of basketball season. Some students did play both sports, as it was with football players going out for basketball, but not without sacrifice. A football player was two or three weeks late in turning out for basketball practice, to the detriment of the team and the frustration of the waiting basketball coach. And Elaine Carter was not one to voluntarily sacrifice anything.

□ 9 □

So much for beginning by seeking the support of Elaine Carter.

The Aldridge High principal, Edson Smalley, might like the idea. A stout man with such boundless energy that he seemed to bounce instead of walk, the principal was constantly calling for new ideas—"breakthroughs," as he put it—to improve life and the educational process at Aldridge High. Well, Jill Winston on the receiving end of Scott Butler's passes certainly qualified as a new idea, a "breakthrough."

Besides, Edson Smalley approved of winning teams. He thought they served to enhance school spirit, and thus enhanced the educational experience for the students. He told Frank exactly that on the day he was hired.

But as principal of Aldridge High, Edson Smalley was a member of the North-Central Conference's Faculty Athletic Board. He probably would feel honor-bound, as a member of the board, to reveal Frank's plan to the board. Not only would that make the plan public, depriving the Panthers of the element of surprise, but it also was sure to send the board into a flap. The board could throw up barriers.

No, much better that the board found out only after— and if—the plan became a fact. And so much better that Edson Smalley found out the same way. The principal would understand. Frank was sure of it.

So much for Edson Smalley as the starting point.

Then suddenly the proper course was crystal clear.

The starting point was obvious: Jill Winston.

So upon arriving at Aldridge High this morning, Frank

checked Jill's schedule and then sent a note to the teacher presiding over the third-period study hall asking her to excuse Jill Winston for a conference in the football coach's office.

"Coach Gardner?"

Frank turned in his chair from the window and in the same motion got to his feet. "Come in, please, Jill."

"You wanted to see me?" She seemed genuinely puzzled.

"Yes, please have a seat," Frank said, gesturing to the wooden chair alongside his desk.

She sat down, an attractive-looking girl with short brown hair and a tanned face, wearing a blouse, jeans, and tennis shoes. She smiled at Frank slightly, waiting.

"Jill," Frank said, "have you ever thought about coming out for football?"

CHAPTER

2

She surprised him.

Watching her face, Frank was expecting an expression of astonishment. Instead he saw her right eyebrow go up slightly, as if weighing her answer to an ordinary, routine question.

Then she smiled at him again.

"You've got to be kidding," she said.

"I'm not kidding," Frank said. He leaned toward her across the desk. "You've got the physical coordination—and the good hands—to become a great pass receiver."

She said nothing.

"I've seen you on the basketball court," Frank said.

"But I—" She stopped without finishing the statement.

"But what?"

"I'm a girl."

"There's nothing in the rule book that says a girl can't be on the team."

She looked past him, through the window. Frank let her have the moment of thought. She hadn't said no. Maybe she was going to say yes.

Then, in that brief moment of silence, all the questions of the summer rolled back through Frank's mind. Was she even interested? Maybe not. Did the possibility of injury worry her? Maybe so. Would her parents stand for it? Maybe not.

And in the course of that brief moment, looking at her, another question entered Frank's mind for the first time: Would Jill Winston want to be identified as a girl who played football, a boys' game—to be teased, perhaps, by male and female friends alike? The question, so unexpected, alarmed Frank. He could think of no ready answer. In the end it might be the most crucial question of all. Why had he not thought of it before?

Frank's heart began to sink. True, she had not responded immediately with a laugh at the ridiculous proposal. She had not issued an immediate rejection. She had not said no. But she was going to do it: say no. Frank was sure of it.

Instead, she said, "I'm on the basketball team."

Frank nodded. "Yes," he said. "A lot of the football players also play basketball."

"Uh-huh," she said slowly. Then she asked, "Have you spoken with Coach Carter about this?"

"No," Frank said. He had anticipated the question and had decided on the simple one-word answer.

"Uh-huh," Jill said again. She again stared past Frank, through the window behind him.

Frank waited, letting her take all the time she wanted. With each passing moment, his sagging hopes rose. She had not blurted out, "Me—a football player? What would everyone say?" If the question entered her mind, she gave no sign of it. Also, he noted with interest, she had not denied her ability, either out of false modesty or honest belief. She seemed to assume that yes, she could do the job. Maybe she had come to that conclusion long ago, watching Eddie McMahon and Lenny Parker drop passes. Was she going to say yes, she wanted to do it? Frank fought down his rising hopes. He was willing to settle for "Let me think about it " or "How quickly do you need to know?"

But she turned to Frank and smiled and said, "My father is going to have a fit."

Frank looked at her a moment. "Does that mean you'd ike to give it a try?"

She shrugged slightly, still smiling. "It sounds like fun." Then she shook her head slightly and repeated, "My father is going to have a fit."

Frank returned her smile. "I'll speak with your father. I can understand that he and your mother will have reservations. But I think I will be able to put their minds at ease. What I have in mind for you carries an almost foolproof guarantee that you won't be hurt. Just sideline and end-zone passes, so you won't be tackled. You'll be in no more danger of injury than you are in on the basketball court. Or in any other sport, for that matter."

She shrugged her shoulders slightly, smiled again, and asked, "Do you know my father?"

"We've never met," Frank said, "but I know who he is."

"Well," she said, with a slight toss of her head, "he's rather definite in his opinions."

"Okay, I've been forewarned. I'll talk to him." Frank got to his feet, and Jill stood. "Do you think this evening—around seven o'clock—would be all right? I could come by your house. If you'd tell your parents that I'm coming—"

"Sure," she said. Then she added, "I'll call you if they've got something planned. But probably they won't on a weeknight. They're usually at home." She gave another grin and Frank thought she was going to repeat her warning—"My father is going to have a fit"—but she said only, "Okay?"

"There's one other thing, Jill."

"Yes?"

"For the time being, this has got to be our secret. Nobody is to know. *Nobody*. Okay?"

Frank half expected Jill to ask about telling Elaine Carter. The girls' basketball coach was so close to her players that it was almost unthinkable that one of them would keep a secret from her.

But Jill asked, "Why?"

"If this works out the way we want it to, you're going to be the Panthers' secret weapon."

Jill nodded. Then she said, Okay."

"You're insane!"

Palmer Winston got to his feet as he spoke the words. He was tall, with broad shoulders and only the first few flecks of gray in his dark brown hair.

Frank remained seated in the overstuffed chair. He almost flinched at Palmer Winston's outburst. He tried to appear calm and even managed a small smile.

He glanced across at Jill's mother, seated next to Jill on a sofa, trying to measure her reaction. The two looked alike, more like sisters than mother and daughter. There was no reaction from either of them.

Then Jill's mother said, "Palmer."

"My daughter—*football*!" Palmer Winston said.

Frank waited, and Mr. Winston, his mouth set in a firm line, finally sat back down and glared—first at Frank, then at his wife and daughter seated together.

"Let me explain," Frank began.

"No, you let me explain. I know men today—strong men—who have bad knees because of football. I was one of the lucky ones. I was never hurt. But a lot of those who *were* hurt—well, they still suffer from the injury years later." He paused. "And you want to expose my daughter to that!"

Frank glanced at Jill, then her mother. Probably they knew, as well as Palmer Winston himself knew, that he was overstating the dangers. True, sometimes players suffered injuries in all sports. But injuries were extremely rare among good athletes playing under able supervision. Mr. and Mrs. Winston surely knew this. They had allowed their son to play football.

"I don't want to expose Jill to any danger at all," Frank said, "and I won't." Frank kept his eyes on Palmer Winston. "If you will hear me out," he said. Palmer Winston waited, not speaking or nodding. Frank continued, "If I thought there was danger of injury to Jill, I would not be sitting here with you now."

Jill's father glared at Frank with his skepticism clearly showing on his face.

"Your daughter is a great athlete. I've seen her on the basketball court. She's got it all, great physical coordination, good strength—and good hands."

"There's quite a bit of difference between playing basketball with girls and playing football with boys," Palmer Winston snapped.

"Yes," Frank said. "But I am not suggesting that Jill make tackles or throw blocks or plunge into the line or try to run through a broken field full of tacklers determined to throw her to the ground."

"But that's football. What's left if you eliminate all that?"

Frank leaned forward slightly. "Passing," he said, and paused. Then he added, "Forward passes."

The answer came right back at Frank. "Pass receivers get tackled."

Frank was still leaning forward. "Not when they catch the ball at the sideline and immediately step out of bounds. Not when they catch the ball in the end zone."

The room was silent a moment.

Frank knew that Palmer Winston saw the point. The man cast a quick glance at his wife, then his daughter. "And you, I assume, really want to do this." It was a statement, not a question.

"Yes," Jill said.

He stared at his daughter a moment. Then he said to her, "I'm not usually one to worry too much about appearances, but"—he hesitated briefly, seeming to shape the words he would speak—"but do you want to be known as a girl who plays football?"

Frank took a quick little breath and waited. The question, when it unexpectedly popped into his mind during his interview with Jill, had alarmed him. Jill had not raised the question. But now her father had.

Jill gave a small laugh, shook her head, and said, "Oh, Dad."

Palmer Winston was waiting for more of an answer.

Mrs. Winston provided the answer. "That's what my father said when I wanted to play basketball in high school: 'Do you want everyone to think of you as a sweaty athlete?' Well, I went ahead and became a sweaty athlete. I enjoyed it." As if underscoring her statement, she added, "And I survived it."

"That was twenty-five years ago," Palmer Winston snapped back.

"And this is today," Mrs. Winston said.

Frank drove from the Winston house to the home of Scott Butler.

He had won Palmer Winston's agreement—unenthusiastic, for sure, even shaky and tentative, but nevertheless an agreement to move ahead. Yes, Jill could begin secret pass-receiving drills. No harm in that. Probably, yes, she could play in a game. They would see how it went. Palmer Winston remained unconvinced on the question of possible injury. He might change his mind at any time.

It was less of a victory than Frank had hoped for. But it was more than he had dared expect after Jill's father had exploded at the first mention. It was, at least, a beginning, and Frank was confident that time and events would erase Palmer Winston's fears.

Now Frank had another selling job to perform—on Scott Butler, his quarterback. Scott should be easy to convince. He was a deadeye passer with a quick release but no talented receivers. He had the ability and the strength to develop into a first-rate college quarterback, and perhaps enough of what it took to move into a professional football career—but no capable receivers at Aldridge High to help him display his talents. He was sure to leap at the opportunity to throw his passes into a pair of hands capable of hanging on to the ball—no matter who owned those hands—and to find himself the quarterback of a winning team instead of a so-so team.

Yes, Scott Butler should be easy to convince.

Frank pulled his car into the Butlers' driveway and got

out. He skipped up the steps of the porch, telling himself to remember that he was delivering good news.

He rang the doorbell. The sound of the soft chime had barely faded away when the door opened.

"Mrs. Butler, how are you?"

"Oh, Coach Gardner. Is anything wrong?"

Frank smiled. "No, but I have something I need to discuss with Scott. Is he home?"

"Yes, come in."

"No, I don't want to disturb your evening. Maybe Scott and I could talk on the porch. It's a team matter, but no problem. Exactly the opposite, I think."

Scott came to the door. "What's up, Coach?"

They walked together across the porch and sat on the top step.

"What's up," Frank said, "is that I think I've found a receiver to give us a passing attack."

"Really? Somebody transfer in? Who is it?"

"Jill Winston."

In the darkness on the porch, Frank could not see Scott's face clearly. But he thought he could almost hear the surprise registering with his quarterback. Scott said nothing for a moment.

Then, "You've got to be kidding."

"That's the second time today I've heard that line," Frank said.

"But—she's a girl!"

"I've heard that line today, too."

"Are you serious?"

"Yes, Scott, I am. I'm very serious. I'm not kidding at all. And yes, I will agree that Jill Winston is a girl." He turned to Scott and could see a faint outline of the handsome face in the darkness. "Most important of all to us, Scott, is that she can catch the ball."

"Coach, I—"

Frank grinned in the darkness. "No, Scott, I haven't gone crazy."

"But Coach, even if she can catch the ball, they'll break her in two. Nobody's more vulnerable than a pass receiver."

"Listen to me for a minute. Then you can tell me that I'm crazy if you want to. But I don't think you will."

Frank laid out his plan. There would be sideline passes with Jill running out of bounds with the ball, out of reach of tacklers. There would be passes into the end zone, where she would not be tackled. There would be no passes across the middle, where she almost certainly would be tackled. And there would not be any long passes downfield that were short of the goal line. She would never be touched. But her catches would produce yards the Panthers currently had no hope of making. And once established as a receiving threat, her mere presence running her patterns would have great decoy value—to the benefit of the runners and even to the benefit of Eddie McMahon going out for passes.

"It'll pay off on all counts," Frank said and paused, resting his case.

"Jeez," Scott said.

"Is that all you've got to say?"

There was a moment of silence. Then, "Maybe it'll work."

When Frank got home, Carol laid down her book, looked up, and asked, "Well?"

"Well, I have a new wide receiver—I think—and a quarterback who agrees—I think—that this is a good idea, and we begin with a drill in the gymnasium tomorrow night—just the three of us."

"The his-and-hers football offense," Carol said.

CHAPTER 3

Frank bent over the football and centered it up into Scott's hands. Then the coach stood up and watched.

Scott, with the ball, backpedaled quickly. Frank gave him hardly a glance. He turned to watch Jill.

Off to the side Jill loped forward for seven strides, cut to her right, and came to a halt just inside the sideline stripe of the basketball court.

By the time she made her cut, the ball was on the way. When she turned, the ball was there. She had her hands up, and the ball plunked into her grip. She tucked the ball away and ran across the sideline stripe to the first row of seats.

"Nice," Frank called out. "Really nice."

Jill grinned at Frank and sent the football back to him with a shovel pass.

The early evening light in the gymnasium was fading

fast. They had only a few more minutes before having to call a halt to the drill because of the advancing darkness. Frank did not dare turn on the arc-lights for fear someone passing by—Elaine Carter? Edson Smalley?— might notice, think something was wrong, and investigate. Frank was not ready to explain why Scott Butler was throwing a football to Jill Winston on the basketball court.

They had begun almost an hour earlier, a few minutes after the last of the players had showered away the dust and sweat of practice, dressed, and left for the day. For the first several minutes of the drill, Ron Matthews stood in the lobby, and then outside, to intercept any player who might be returning for a word with Frank. Sometimes the players liked to speak alone with the coach, and after practice was the best time. But not on this day.

Frank spent the first few minutes explaining the simple patterns he wanted Jill to run—seven strides forward, cut to the sideline stripe, stop, catch the ball, run out of bounds.

Jill nodded through it all, smiling in anticipation.

Frank got a bonus at the end of his explanation when he suggested that Scott and Jill spend a few minutes tossing the ball back and forth to give Jill a bit of the feel of the oval shape. Catching a football wasn't the same as catching a basketball.

"That's not necessary," Jill said. "I've played touch football a lot. I've caught passes before."

But as it turned out, Jill had not caught varsity-caliber bullet passes before.

Scott, perhaps unconsciously taking into account the fact that he was throwing to a girl, floated softies out to Jill, and she grabbed them easily.

"Fire it in there," Frank said. "This isn't a Sunday school game."

Scott gave Frank a questioning look, then nodded.

Ron, standing inside the door for a moment with his arms folded before taking another precautionary walk outside, watched with an expression of utter disbelief on his face.

Jill bobbled and dropped the first bullet pass, then let the second zip through her hands. Returning to her position for the next pass, she said, "I'll get the hang of it."

And she did. As if she had made some adjustment in her reflexes, she threw up her hands quicker, grabbed quicker, and hung on to the ball—once, then again, then a third time. On the fourth pass, Scott overthrew her. She caught the fifth and sixth passes.

Frank switched her to a crossing pattern, such as she might run in the end zone. First she took short passes over center. Then she went after passes in the corner. She caught seven of eight over center. Scott missed her on two in the corner, but she caught four of the other five.

Scott began grinning with each catch.

Ron, watching from a sideline, was changing his expression from disbelief to belief.

"Let's do one more crossover, and then we'll call it a day," Frank said. "It's getting too dark."

"I can see okay," Jill said. She seemed to be enjoying herself.

"No, this will be enough for today," Frank said. He did not want to take a chance on one of Scott's whistling passes getting lost for a second in a shadow and hitting her in the face.

She caught the last pass of the day, and Frank walked outside with Ron and Scott and Jill, locking the door behind him.

"See you tomorrow," Jill said with a wave, and headed toward a car parked at the curb.

Ron said, "I've got to admit it—mighty impressive."

Frank turned to Scott. "Well?"

Scott shrugged slightly. "She's good," he said. Then he added, "I've never thrown to anyone that good."

Frank nodded.

"Maybe it'll work," Scott said.

Frank turned and looked at Scott. "Is that all?"

"It'd sure be better if she was a boy."

Frank laughed. "You can't have everything."

"Coach, I've got a problem."

Jill Winston stood in the door to Frank's office.

The bell had just rung, ending the second class period of the day. Jill should have been on her way to the study hall, from where Frank had summoned her three days before.

"Come in," Frank said. He stood up and walked around his desk. His first thought put a frown on his face: Palmer Winston, having thought things over for a couple of days, had decided against a high school football career for his daughter.] "Come in and sit down," Frank said. He walked past her and closed the office door. "What is it?"

Jill sat down on a wooden chair, and Frank returned to his seat. He said again, "What is it?"

Jill looked at the floor a moment, her lips pursed a bit, and said, "I have to talk to you—I mean, without Scott."

"All right."

The bell rang, signaling the start of the third class period. "Will you write me an excuse for being late to study hall? This is going to take a few minutes, I'm afraid."

Frank did not like the idea. He had summoned her from the study hall on Monday. That one instance was taking a chance on letting the secret out even before there was a secret. The study hall teacher might well have thought it unusual for the football coach to summon Jill Winston, and make mention of the fact. If the word reached Elaine Carter, there were sure to be questions. But the chance had to be taken. It was unavoidable. And apparently Frank had won the gamble. There had been no inquiry from Elaine Carter or anyone else.

But now, to request that she be excused a second time in the same week, the risk was multiplied.

But Frank said, "Sure, of course." He had no choice.

Jill nodded and said nothing for a moment, seeming to search for the right words.

"You said there is a problem," Frank prodded.

"It's Henry."

"Henry?" Frank frowned. Then he recalled seeing Jill

walking in the corridors with Henry Allison. Henry played right tackle on offense for the Panthers. He was a senior, big, strong, and fast, sure to make an outstanding lineman for some college team. "Henry Allison?" Frank asked, puzzled. "What does Henry have to do with all this?"

"Well . . ."

Frank waited.

"Well, Henry and I sort of go steady, you know."

Frank thought he saw what was coming next but said nothing.

"Well, Henry usually comes by the house for a little while—you know, in the evening after football practice. But on Monday night I told him not to come, that I had something to do. You know, you were coming to talk to my folks. And then these last two nights, he's come by and, well, I wasn't there. My folks told him that I'd gone somewhere in the car, which was true, and probably would be back pretty soon. Well, that was okay for one night—but the second night . . . and then there'll be tonight . . ."

"I see," Frank said.

"It's kind of a problem," Jill said.

"Yes." Frank thought a minute. Then he said, "Jill, can Henry keep a secret?"

She didn't hesitate. "I think so. Yes."

Frank nodded. "Then go ahead and tell him what's up. But please make sure he understands the importance of this remaining confidential for the time being. I'll talk to him, too."

Jill made no move to go. "Well, there's something else," she said.

"Oh?"

Again, Jill said nothing for a moment, appearing to search for the right words. Then she said, "I don't think Henry would like the idea very much of my spending an hour every evening with Scott. I—"

Frank felt a small twinge of alarm. "Is there some problem between them—Scott and Henry?" Frank did not like the idea of trouble between two of his starters.

"No, no. It's not that. It's just that Henry sometimes . . ." She let the sentence trail off.

"Henry sometimes is a little jealous, even when he doesn't need to be," Frank finished for her. "Is that it?"

"Yes, sort of."

"Okay," Frank said. "If Henry is going to know what's up, he might as well join us in the drills. Do you think that will fix things?"

She smiled. "Yes," she said. "Would that be okay?"

"Sure," Frank said.

Frank wrote her a note excusing her tardiness in the study hall and watched her go, grateful that the problem had been Henry Allison instead of Palmer Winston.

But Frank's sense of relief lasted only until the lunch period.

As he moved through the cafeteria line with his tray, he felt like smiling at everyone, and he did—the faculty and staff members and the students he knew. If he had been alone, he might have hummed a tune or thrown his hands into the air and shouted, "Hurrah!" The world was beginning to look like a bright and happy place.

Only three days ago he was facing the prospect of a dismal season for his Panthers, with only a remote idea in the back of his mind offering the slightest hope of improvement.

Now, three days later, the click of events had transformed Frank's frown into a grin and had improved the Panthers' prospects for the coming season from hopelessly mediocre to bright if not brilliant.

First Jill had said yes. Then her parents had said yes—well, at least a yes to passing drills, and they hadn't said no to playing in a game. Then Scott Butler had said yes. The drills in the gymnasium showed almost immediately that Jill had every bit the talent Frank had expected. The only hint of a problem so far—Henry Allison—had been solved easily. And the only hint of a problem in the future—Jill's parents deciding to say no—seemed to diminish with each passing day.

In his mind Frank already could see Jill in a game, loping forward, then looping over toward the sideline, and taking in a pass as she stepped out of bounds.

The world indeed was shaping up as a beautiful place.

Frank paid the cashier and walked with his tray toward the faculty table at the far side of the cafeteria. To his left he spotted Henry and Jill seated across from each other, alone at the end of one of the long tables. Henry's back was to him. Jill's face wore a frown as she listened to something Henry was saying. Undoubtedly they were discussing the reason for Jill's absence from home the last two evenings, and the offer for Henry to join in the secret drills.

Frank walked on toward the faculty dining table without giving them another glance. The secret was spreading, by his consent, and he did not want to take a chance on revealing anything through chance remarks or knowing glances.

Frank had just seated himself alongside Mr. Crain, an algebra teacher, when he saw Jill, eyes straight ahead, her face fixed in a mixture of anger and determination, stalk past alone.

He watched her leave the cafeteria and then glanced across to the table where she had been seated. Henry was sitting there alone. Then, as Frank watched, Henry got up and moved to a table where several football players were eating.

Frank was no longer smiling. He did not feel like humming a tune or throwing his hands into the air and shouting "Hurrah!" Instead, he frowned, ate his lunch as quickly as possible, and left.

CHAPTER

4

Jill was seated on the wooden chair in Frank's office when he walked in. Frank glanced at the clock on the wall. The lunch hour had fifteen minutes to go. Jill's expression reminded him of clouds in the sky moments before a thunderstorm struck. He closed the door and walked to his chair, asking, "What's wrong?"

"Everything," she said.

"Henry?" he suggested.

"Henry," she said and stopped, her mouth a straight line. "Henry doesn't want me to do it."

"Why?" Frank asked. He was afraid he knew the answer. It was that same alarming question—a *girl* football player? He should have anticipated Henry Allison's reaction. He should have spoken to Henry himself. Too late now. All that remained was a repair job—find out what went wrong and try to fix it. Frank sighed in the moment of silence, waiting for Jill's answer. He reflected that he was new to the business of patching up romance problems on his football team.

Jill took a deep breath and exhaled with an expression of complete exasperation on her face. "He says he will become the joke of the school having a girlfriend who plays football." She snapped the words out. "He says he doesn't want to go steady with a member of the football team."

Frank tried to read Jill's thoughts, in the expression on her face, in the tone of her voice. She appeared more determined than troubled. She sounded angry.

"And what do *you* think?" Frank asked. "That's more important right now than what Henry thinks."

Anger flashed in her eyes. "I think, I think . . . How dare he think he can order me around like that. I have a right—"

Frank smiled and waved a hand, and she stopped in mid-sentence. Her expression still reminded him of storm clouds. The strong-willed girl who competed so fiercely on the basketball court, and now was ready to compete on a football field, wasn't going to be shoved around by Henry Allison. That was good. But still, there was a problem. And, left alone, the problem was sure to get worse. "Okay, okay," Frank said.

Jill watched him without speaking.

"I'll talk to Henry," Frank said. "It'll be okay."

She said nothing for a moment. Then, "I don't know. He was really . . ." She let the sentence trail off. The anger in her eyes softened.

□ 33 □

Frank, watching the change in her face, waited for her to continue. He knew the question that was coming next. He could almost hear the words forming in the silence between them.

"Do you think," she finally asked, "that everyone will tease Henry if I play football?"

That, Frank decided, was the question that had brought her into his office. She had not come to ask him to speak with Henry. And she had not, it appeared, come to tell Frank she was bowing to Henry's protests and giving up the project. She was concerned about the risk of subjecting her boyfriend to ridicule.

"In all honesty," Frank said, speaking slowly, "yes, there may be some wisecrack, some joke—but just one. If there is one, I can guarantee you that there won't be a second one."

Jill stared past him out the window, thinking, as she had done on the morning he first proposed football to her. "My father, you know, said sort of the same thing— did I want to be known as a girl who played football." She spoke the words softly, as if she was talking to herself instead of to Frank.

"Jill, let me say two things. First and most important, if anything at all about this idea bothers you—Henry's objections, what people may think or say, anything at all—if it bothers you, let's drop it right now. It's up to you."

"No, I—"

"Let me finish."

She nodded.

"And second, you should know that your role on the football team would be that of a skilled performer. There is nothing unfeminine, unladylike, about athletic skill. The world is full of talented, skilled women athletes, and nobody teases them or their boyfriends about it. That is what I am going to tell Henry, and that is what I think you should tell Henry or anyone else."

She was nodding her head slightly again as he finished.

"If you want to go ahead and do it, that is," he said and waited.

She looked at him and said, "Okay."

"Okay? Okay what?"

She smiled at him. "I'm going to do it. I want to do it, and I'm *going* to do it."

"I'll talk to Henry," Frank said.

"So will I," Jill added.

That afternoon, when Henry Allison turned the corner and headed down the corridor toward the dressing room, Frank was waiting for him.

In the two hours that had passed since Jill left his office, Frank realized that he had more than Henry's objections to discuss with the big tackle. The picture of Henry Allison moving over to the cafeteria table with the football players kept reappearing in Frank's mind. In the wake of the argument with Jill, had Henry told his teammates about her? Was the news now spreading through the corridors of Aldridge High?

But Frank, as he headed for the meeting with Henry,

had not heard from an outraged Elaine Carter. He had not heard from a curious Edson Smalley. He had not received an alarmed report from Scott Butler about what everyone was saying. It appeared that Henry had not spread the secret. He hoped not.

"Henry, do you have a minute?" Frank said.

Henry grinned sheepishly. He did not seem surprised. "Sure," he said and followed the coach to his office.

Frank closed the door behind him, but he neither took a seat nor offered one to Henry. This was going to be a short interview. Frank turned to the boy. "What's this Jill is telling me about you objecting to her catching passes for the Panthers?"

Henry shuffled his feet and stared at the floor. "Aw, it's all right, Coach," he said finally.

"What do you mean, all right? She said you objected."

"Well, yeah. But we've talked about it. No problem." He looked at Frank. "She told me you were going to talk to me about it."

"You're afraid people will tease you about having a girlfriend who plays football?"

Henry smiled. "Yeah," he said. He paused, then added, "And they will."

Frank looked Henry up and down—all six feet, five inches of him—and said, "I think you're big enough to handle anything like that."

"Yeah, I am."

Frank watched him closely. "Then we're okay," he said, stating a fact rather than asking a question.

"Sure," Henry said. "Like I said, we've talked—Jill and I—and it's okay." He gave another sheepish grin. "I knew all along that she'd talk me out of it, or you would."

Frank waited a second, then said, "All right."

He turned to open the door, then stopped. The question popped back into his mind: Had Henry told anyone? Frank left the door closed, his hand on the knob, and asked, "Have you said anything to anyone—*anyone*—about this?"

"No. Jill said it was supposed to be a secret."

Frank almost smiled but kept his mouth straight. Henry Allison had known even as he was protesting that Jill was going to go ahead and that he would accept it. "Good," Frank said.

He opened the door and let Henry lead the way to the dressing room.

So the threesome became a foursome in the gymnasium in the week leading up to the opening game.

Frank gradually introduced different pass patterns into the routine, some of which Jill might run without ever receiving a pass. They left her too vulnerable to a tackle if she received the ball. But they were valuable patterns for her to run as a decoy, and she needed to understand them as well as the ones in which she was the primary receiver. Eventually, of course, teams would discover that no passes were going to Jill in the middle of the field, and her value as a decoy there would diminish. But in her first game or two, no opponent would be able to assume with safety that she was a decoy and nothing more.

Henry turned out to be an asset in the drills on the gymnasium floor. Playing the role of defensive back, he chased Jill through the patterns, trying to knock away the passes.

To Frank's delight, Henry found little success. Jill had long since learned in basketball the value of shoulder fakes and hip fakes to gain a brief second—but enough— of opening. And she had long since mastered the art of catching a pass with an opponent's waggling hands in front of her face.

With every running of a pattern, Jill became more sure of her steps. Perhaps again drawing on her basketball experience, she seemed instinctively to know where the sideline was, without wasting a glance at her feet, and stopped just inside every time. And with every pass from Scott, she gained confidence in the ability of her hands to capture and hold the rifling ball.

And Scott, for his part, grew more confident in his receiver with every pass. He threw the ball with all the strength, all the zip, he ever applied to a pass to any other receiver. Increasingly, as Scott brought his arm down from sending a pass on its way, his face showed the expression that a quarterback wears when he expects his pass to be caught.

Frank knew that Scott's confidence was no less important than Jill's, and he caught himself smiling increasingly as they passed and caught their way through the second week of the secret drills.

Twice during that week Frank left his office at Aldridge High at mid-morning and visited Palmer Winston in his law office.

In the first visit, he wanted to take the temperature of the situation, measure the mood of Jill Winston's reluctant father, and reassure himself that, after all, the answer was going to be yes. He described the drills in detail, praised Jill's talents, emphasized again and again the restrictions guaranteeing Jill's safety, and invited him to attend the drills any time.

Palmer Winston let slide Frank's invitation to the drills and then surprised Frank with his next comment.

"Henry says there's not a chance of Jill being hit," he said.

A bit uncertainly Frank said, "Oh?" He wondered what his right tackle had been saying around the Winston household about the drills. Then it occurred to Frank that maybe the interested father had been questioning Henry, as well as his daughter.

"Henry says there's not been a single pass where he could have legally tackled Jill."

"It's planned that way," Frank said cautiously.

Mr. Winston sat behind his desk and looked at Frank. "Could she be illegally tackled—a foul?"

Frank returned Mr. Winston's stare. "Yes, of course," he said. "Of course it could happen. But it's highly unlikely, *extremely* unlikely." He paused, then added, "You and I both know it's possible. Things do happen sometimes. But it's rare, very rare. The officials won't allow it. Beyond that, the coaches themselves won't stand for it." He watched Palmer Winston and then asked, "How many times did you see an illegal hit out of bounds when you were playing?"

Palmer Winston said only, "Umm," and Frank eventually departed, having to be satisfied with the fact that while there had been no definite yes, there also had not been a no.

On the second visit Frank knew he had to obtain a yes—or accept a no. He carried with him the standard Aldridge High release form. Signed by a parent, the form released the school from any responsibility in the event of injury to a student taking part in a school activity Palmer Winston had signed the form before—for his son to play football, for Jill to play basketball.

Would he sign a form for Jill to play football?

Mr. Winston took the form, glanced at it, looked up at Frank, and then signed.

"Thank you," Frank said, smiling.

Palmer Winston did not smile. He shook his head slightly and said, "She's a very determined girl. We've always told her to make up her own mind about things. She made up her mind about this. If her safety's not at stake"—he gave Frank a sharp glance—"and everyone but me seems sure it's not—then I can't say no to her."

———

By the evening of Thursday's drill, the night before the Panthers' season-opening game, Frank considered Jill to be ready, and he told her so.

They were standing at the door of the gymnasium—Frank, Scott, Jill, and Henry—preparing to leave.

"But I'm not going to play you tomorrow night," Frank said. "Not even going to dress you out."

Jill, who had laughed and joked her way through the passing drill and then had smiled with eyes sparkling while listening to Frank tell her she was ready, almost took a step backward, and her expression went flat. "Why—?"

"Remember when we first talked and I told you that you were going to be the Panthers' secret weapon? Remember, I said that was one reason we had to keep this a secret?"

"Yes, I remember."

"Jill, we're not going to need our secret weapon tomorrow night. You know about Johnson City. They're not going to be any problem. They're smaller than we are, and not so good—the perfect season opener, a good warm-up." He paused. "And if we play you—then the secret isn't a secret any longer. We will have given away our surprise, without needing to give it away. I'd rather keep the secret weapon a secret until it's needed—against Randville next week."

Frank understood the disappointment written all over Jill's face. She had brought herself to a peak and was ready to play. Frank liked seeing her bringing herself to a peak. It helped sharpen the drills, stepped up her progress.

Frank said, "Our second game, well, that's something else. The Randville Tigers were conference champions last year. It looks like they're loaded again. That's the game to unveil our secret weapon."

Jill nodded her head in resignation and said, "Okay."

CHAPTER

5

But the Johnson City Trojans quickly gave Frank cause to wish that Jill Winston was standing on the sideline, in uniform, ready to go into the game, instead of watching the game from somewhere up in the grandstands. The opening minutes were a horror almost without equal in Frank's coaching career.

First the Trojans stopped the Panthers cold in their first possession, forcing a punt on fourth down. Their reckless blitzing—daring Scott to throw a pass— knocked the quarterback off balance and nailed the Panthers' runners in their tracks.

Then, after a twenty-yard punt return put them on the Panthers' thirty-one-yard line, the Trojans marched to the end zone and scored in seven plays.

On the field, and along the sideline across the field, the underdog Trojans whooped it up, celebrating the startling fact that they had stopped the Panthers and then scored.

Frank knew well the dangers of such an infusion of confidence in an underdog.

He knew, too, the dangers to his own team, confident of victory in a tune-up season opener, now finding themselves stalled on offense and run over on defense. The reckless blitzing had worked, stopping the Panthers. Nothing flattened the spirit of defensive players like a sputtering offense. It meant that their hard work went for naught.

Clearly a depressed Panthers' offense had come off the field, to be replaced by a doubting defense. In both units there were too many memories of last year's mediocre performance.

As if the Panthers were due some sort of consolation, the Trojans failed in their kick for the extra point because of a bad snap from center.

With the game barely five minutes old, Johnson City led Aldridge High, 6–0, and the home-field grandstands were silent.

In the Panthers' second possession, Scott passed on first down, a quick opener over center, above the heads of the linebackers charging in on him, to Eddie McMahon. Eddie hung on for an eight-yard gain.

On the sideline Frank nodded his approval. The play was worth much more than the eight yards gained. The Johnson City defenders might have come into the game knowing the Panthers lacked the ingredients of an effective passing attack. But now they had learned that an occasional completion was not impossible. Eddie, with just one more step, would have been free to sprint to the end zone. The pass was a close call for the Johnson City defenders. They would be displaying a little caution now.

The Panthers, with Richie Fields running inside and Marty Elmore skirting the ends, moved to midfield against a Johnson City defense that was, indeed, more cautious. But then Richie hit a brick wall for no gain trying to go off tackle. A pass to Lenny Parker failed. And Marty got tripped up after only three yards on a wide sweep.

The Panthers punted deep into Johnson City territory.

The Trojans' offense, seeming to sense that things were going to be different this time, took the field not with cheers but with grim, businesslike faces.

The Panthers' defense, to Frank's satisfaction, took the field with the same grim, businesslike faces and forced the Trojans to punt after three plays.

The game settled into a struggle between the thirty-yard lines.

The Panthers were able to move the ball, but only in spurts. Twice draw plays produced big gainers, one for twelve yards, the other for fourteen. Lenny Parker caught a pass for nine yards. Richie was a strong runner into the line, and Marty was quick around the ends. But the Panthers were not able to put together the gainers into a drive to a touchdown.

What the Panthers needed was a sure-fire pass receiver—pass receptions on order. Once, Frank caught himself unconsciously turning and scanning the quiet crowd in the grandstand behind the bench. The receiver the Panthers needed was up there somewhere.

On the field, the Panthers' defense had stiffened. There was no semblance of another Johnson City drive to the end zone. At the halftime, the score remained 6–0.

"We'll wear 'em down," Frank told the players in the dressing room. The Trojans were generally smaller than the Panthers, and they had fewer reserves. The Trojans were going to be a tired bunch in the fourth quarter. The first signs of weariness already were beginning to show. "Just hang in there, give 'em lots of physical contact, don't let 'em have another touchdown, and we'll win this game in the second half. The second half belongs to us."

Frank got a lot of uncertain looks in return.

The Panthers won the game in the fourth quarter. A tiring Johnson City ball carrier fumbled the ball when he was tackled, and the Panthers' nose guard, Georgie Francis, fell on it on the Trojans' twenty-one-yard line.

Frank clapped his hands and shouted as Scott led the offensive unit onto the field. Now or never, he figured.

Scott alternated Marty running wide and Richie plunging into the line. The weary Johnson City defenders surrendered yardage each time, and Scott scored the touchdown on a quarterback sneak from the three-yard line.

Denny Hoyt kicked well, enabling the Panthers to escape with a 7–6 triumph.

When Frank walked out of the dressing room behind

the last player, Carol greeted him with "I think your offense needed the woman's touch."

Frank looked at Carol and managed his first smile in more than two hours.

On Saturday morning Frank drove to the school to view the game tapes and conduct his ritual day-after-the-game interview with Boots Sheridan, sports editor of the *Aldridge Morning Herald*. Frank dreaded facing the sardonic gaze and the blunt questions of the sports editor.

Boots Sheridan was a lifelong resident of Aldridge, except for the four years he spent away at college. He joined the *Morning Herald* sports staff after graduation and shortly afterward became sports editor—some twenty years ago.

In their first meeting, on the day of the announcement of Frank's appointment, Boots made clear that he considered himself the final arbiter of Aldridge High athletics. He decided what was good and what wasn't, and told the people of Aldridge about it in his articles in the *Morning Herald*. In that first meeting with Frank, Boots raised an eyebrow and let Frank know that his critical articles had been a major factor in sending Frank's predecessor packing.

The message was clear: Boots Sheridan expected Frank Gardner to satisfy Boots Sheridan. Or else.

All through Frank's first season of five victories and five losses, Boots repeatedly told Frank—and several times wrote in the paper—that nobody was expecting a miracle the first year.

Again the message was clear: After one year there had better be some success, with or without miracles.

Now, one day after a squeaky 7–6 victory over little Johnson City in the first game of the second season, Frank was meeting with the sports editor to discuss the game, and Frank did not relish the idea.

Approaching the school, passing by the tennis courts next to the stadium, Frank barely noticed the two players volleying in warm-up. His mind was on other things—the Trojans' surprising drive for a touchdown in their first possession, a bullet pass that skittered through Lenny Parker's hands, the pleasing evidence of Richie Fields' improved running, and, with a frown, the upcoming session with Boots Sheridan.

Then something clicked in Frank's mind—a small signal to the brain picked up out of the corner of his eye—and he turned his face toward the tennis court. At the same time he pulled the car to the curb and slowed to a stop. He sat watching a moment.

Jill Winston was charging the net. Across from her, playing deep, Henry Allison cocked his arm and prepared to swat the ball bouncing in front of him.

Henry swung through on the ball and sent a cannonball drive to Jill's left. Jill, a righthander, pivoted and leaped, her racquet stretched out. She got the racquet in front of the ball. With a flick of her wrist she put power into the return shot. The ball rocketed back across the net and hit the court a half dozen inches inside the line, well beyond the lunging Henry and his outstretched racquet.

Frank heard Henry call out, "Nice shot."

Jill was grinning.

Frank got out of his car and walked to the chainlink fence surrounding the courts.

"Hey, Coach," Henry said.

"Good morning."

Henry and Jill walked to the fence.

"You think this is wise?" Frank asked. "We don't want our secret weapon to sprain an ankle." He turned to Henry. "Nor our right tackle, either."

They both looked surprised.

"A sprained ankle?" Jill asked in a puzzled tone, as if Frank were referring to something completely outside the realm of possibility. "I've never had a sprained ankle in my life."

Probably true, Frank thought. Jill Winston was an outstanding athlete, always active, always in shape, always able to control her body. She wasn't the kind to sprain an ankle.

"Me either, Coach," Henry chimed in.

"Okay," Frank said. "I'm not going to tell you not to play tennis. But do be careful. Take it easy. Don't take any chances. Okay?"

"Sure," they both said at the same time.

Frank nodded and repeated, "Okay, but be careful." Then he returned to his car.

Frank had resolved years before, when he himself was a high school athlete, not to be one of those football coaches who insisted that the world revolved around football and nothing else. Frank's own coach had done it, restricting the football players' athletic endeavors to football alone, and Frank had resented it.

On occasion Frank had been tempted to interfere with a player's outside activities. There had been the time a running back had entered a diving competition at the municipal pool during the summer. But he had stuck to his rule.

And he stuck to it this time, leaving Henry and Jill on the tennis court.

But he was frowning as he drove the car away from the curb, toward the faculty and staff parking slots next to the field house.

Boots Sheridan arrived just as, on the screen, the Panthers' Georgie Francis was recovering a Johnson City fumble on the twenty-one-yard line, setting the stage for the game-winning touchdown.

Except for Johnson City's touchdown drive in the opening minutes, Frank had run the tape almost nonstop. He needed to study the flaws in the Aldridge High defense that had allowed the Trojans to move downfield to the end zone. The first defensive series of the Panthers' season had been a disaster. Frank needed to know the details of the problem, even though the defense had shaped up and played well the rest of the game. He did not want a repeat in some future game.

As for the rest of the game, the plays—each block, each tackle, each run, each pass—were so deeply etched in Frank's brain that he needed only to review the action.

He knew the problem on offense—the lack of an effective passing attack—and he jotted down the instances when a pass completion either would have kept a drive alive or would have spread out the defense to set up the running game. There were eight such situations jotted down in pencil on the legal-size pad of yellow paper when he heard Boots Sheridan's voice from behind him.

"Just looking at the good part, I see," Boots said.

Frank turned and nodded a greeting and switched off the machine. "The only good part," he conceded.

"Yeah, the only good part," Boots said, watching Frank and waiting for a response.

"Let's go in my office," Frank said. "We can talk there."

Frank led the sports editor out of the training room and down the corridor to his office and took a seat behind his desk. Boots settled into the chair next to the desk.

"Shoot," Frank said, reflecting that that probably was precisely the right word in this situation with Boots Sheridan.

"You're lucky that was Johnson City and not, for example, the Randville Tigers, who are coming along next week."

Frank gave Boots a tight little smile. "Is that a question?" he asked.

"No, it's a statement of fact. Do you agree with it?"

"I'll agree that we certainly could have lost the game. It was closer than I like them to be."

"But against Johnson City . . ." Boots said and let the words trail off in a tone of disbelief. "And now with Randville . . ." He let the words trail off again, implying some sort of unspeakable horror approaching over the horizon.

"The Trojans played well," Frank said, determined not to allow Boots to lead him into speculation on the upcoming Randville game. "They gave us a real tussle."

Boots leaned forward, seeming set on not letting Frank off the hook. "What are you going to do to keep the Randville Tigers from blowing you all the way out of the county, not to mention the stadium, next week?"

Frank leaned back in his chair and stared past Boots for a moment.

There were a lot of answers to that question. For one thing, with any luck at all, the Randville Tigers at this very moment were taking a very large step toward overconfidence. They were going to be playing the Aldridge High Panthers, who had barely escaped defeat at the hands of tiny and lowly Johnson City. For another thing, the Randville Tigers now had clear evidence that the Panthers, same as last year, did not have a passing attack. The Tigers were sure to work all week against stopping the run. Why worry about passes? Frank almost smiled at the chaos the first two or three passes to Jill Winston would cause in the Randville secondary.

But Frank gave none of these answers to Boots. Instead, he leaned forward and said, "Boots, I'm going to level with you."

"Please do," Boots said with a tinge of sarcasm. "I can hardly wait."

"The straight story is that I am not going to tell you what I am going to do," Frank said. "For one thing, I'm afraid the Randville coaches know how to read."

Boots appeared neither surprised nor offended. To the

contrary, he appeared almost satisfied by what he obviously interpreted as a simple matter of Frank ducking a question for lack of having an answer. "That means," he said, "that you don't know what you're going to do about Randville, is that it?"

In eight years of coaching at small high schools, Frank had had few dealings with sportswriters beyond the hometown reporters, most of them friendlier than Boots. But Frank was able to recognize the old reporter's trick of throwing out a question as a challenge in an effort to provoke an unintended reply. Frank was now supposed to leap to his own defense and reveal more than he wanted to reveal.

Boots waited with something akin to a sneer on his face.

When Frank said nothing immediately, Boots went on. "Fact is, you've failed to develop a passing attack, even though you've got the best passer in the conference in Scott Butler. You've failed to teach someone—Lenny or Eddie or someone—how to be a good receiver." He paused. "And now comes Randville. What are you going to do?"

Frank managed a small, patient smile at the sports editor. For a moment he mused over what Boots Sheridan would say if Frank told him about Jill Winston. Maybe Boots would fall off the chair. That would be a funny sight. Or maybe he would involuntarily rise to his feet while his mouth dropped open. That, too, would be a funny sight.

Frank brought himself back to the present. He would

have to forgo for the time being the pleasure of shocking Boots Sheridan into falling off his chair or standing up with his mouth agape.

The reporter would have to wait until Friday night to find out about Jill Winston, along with the rest of the world. Then Boots could fall off his chair, or stand up with his mouth dropping open, or whatever he liked.

"Let's talk about the facts of the Johnson City game," Frank said. "I'm not much for speculation about future games."

For Frank the rest of the weekend around town seemed an unending rerun of Boots Sheridan's questions: If the Panthers had all that trouble eking out a victory over little Johnson City, what was going to happen against the powerful Randville Tigers?

The question kept coming at Frank from all directions. He heard the question in a consoling telephone call from an interested Edson Smalley. He heard it from the barber cutting his hair. He heard it twice in a restaurant on Saturday night, when he and Carol went out to eat. He heard the question on Sunday afternoon from a total stranger behind him in a line at the shopping mall.

Frank's answer always was the same: "It's a problem. We're working on it. We'll have to wait and see."

CHAPTER

6

"We've got a surprise for the Randville Tigers tonight," Frank said. "And it'll come as a surprise to you, too. We're going to do something different. Something new."

Frank was standing in the middle of the dressing room. Around him the faces of forty-one players, wearing the home-game red uniforms with white trim, were turned toward him. The time was almost at hand to take the field for the kickoff against the Randville Tigers.

Frank paused a moment to let his words sink in. The room was silent. Frank looked around at the players. The faces staring back at him were serious and determined. Some of them showed a trace of curiosity at his announcement of something new. But none of the faces showed an oversupply of confidence. After the scare against the Johnson City Trojans, the powerhouse Randville Tigers appeared doubly awesome.

Victory in the end over the Trojans had done little to relieve the chilling reality that Johnson City—a smaller school, an easy opening-game opponent—had been able to stop the Panthers' offense time and again.

The aftereffects of the realization had shown up almost immediately on the practice field. In the Monday drill the players, clearly troubled, were listless, lethargic, without pep. There was none of the cheering, laughing, and good-natured needling of a team that is preparing itself for victory. The Panthers had stumbled through to five victories and five losses in the previous year, a poor season. And now this season looked to be as bad, possibly worse.

Frank tried to fight the practice lethargy by driving the players to harder and harder work. The way out of a slump, Frank knew, was hard work. And a slump was exactly what the Johnson City Trojans had sent the Panthers into in the first game of the season.

But there was little progress. No matter how hard the Panthers ran and blocked and tackled on the practice field, the fact remained that they had no reliable pass receivers. Without the threat of a passing attack, the runners were doomed. And without the runners having a chance, how were the Panthers to score? Without scoring, how were they to win?

The sluggishness of the Panthers on the practice field, their listlessness in pushing themselves through their drills, did not go unnoticed by Boots Sheridan. His practiced eye, sharpened through more than twenty years of watching the Panthers practice from the sidelines, picked up all the telltale signs.

"You've got more of a problem than I thought," he told Frank.

Frank nodded and said only, "We're working on it."

Boots, of course, did more than tell Frank about the Panthers' obvious problem. He told the readers of the *Morning Herald:* "The Panthers' weak showing against the Johnson City Trojans has left the team flatter than a fritter, down in the dumps, and slogging through one of the worst practice weeks this observer can recall seeing at the Aldridge High practice field."

Frank read the words in the newspaper while sipping a cup of coffee at the breakfast table. He was not surprised. The honeymoon period of last year was behind them. Boots Sheridan was wasting no time in this young season issuing demands and criticisms.

From the standpoint of a coach trying to spring a surprise, Boots Sheridan's words in the *Morning Herald* weren't all bad. Matter of fact, they were helpful in one way. If the words reached Randville—and they surely would—they would serve to puff up the Tigers' overconfidence and reinforce the assumption that Aldridge High had no passing attack. The net effect could be points scored for the Panthers.

But Frank knew that his players, and their families and friends, read Boots Sheridan's comments in the *Morning Herald*. He knew from his own experience—first as a player, then as a coach—that it was no fun having your troubles spelled out in the newspaper. Boots Sheridan's words were not going to help the spirit of the Panthers.

On Thursday a worried Scott Butler appeared in Frank's office before practice and said, "Maybe we ought to reveal the secret weapon to the team. You know, have Jill out there on the practice field today. Let everyone see that she can catch passes."

The same thought had occurred to Frank before Monday's practice session was a half-hour old. Ron Matthews had even mentioned, without pressing, that the sight of Jill snagging Scott's bullet passes would give the team a tremendous lift. But Frank discarded the idea as quickly as it had entered his mind. And he let Ron's suggestion go by without comment. To be sure, there were solid advantages in convincing the players that there was a real hope for a balanced offense—a passing attack to go with the running attack. But there were drawbacks in revealing the Jill Winston secret.

Frank cited one of the drawbacks in responding to Scott's urging. "And there would go the element of surprise," he told Scott. "The Johnson City game proved to the Randville scouts that we don't have an effective passing attack. It's important for Randville to think that all week, right up to game time. It's important that all of their defensive plans and all of their practice be based on the claim—false—that we can't move the ball in the air."

But in Frank's mind another drawback loomed even larger. The Jill Winston secret, when known, was sure to set off a series of explosions for miles around. At least one of these explosions was going to occur at Aldridge High—in Elaine Carter's office. Probably another in Edson Smalley's office. If the secret were revealed in advance, there also was sure to be an explosion at Randville High. Wilson Nutting, their volatile coach, would blow sky-high as a matter of policy. He would file a protest, for sure, determined to deprive the Panthers of any weapon they might use against the Tigers. And the North-Central Conference's Offices would be thrown into turmoil, faced with a dilemma without precedent.

Frank did not want those explosions to occur on the day before the game. In the midst of all those explosions, someone might come up with a reason for holding Jill out of the game.

Now, though, with the opening kickoff only a few minutes away, the time had come to tell the Aldridge High players—and then everyone in the stadium—that Jill Winston, a girl, was going to be catching passes for the Aldridge High Panthers.

Frank glanced at his wristwatch. Jill, who had changed into her game uniform in Frank's office, would be outside in the corridor, waiting for him to open the door.

"It's time to let you in on a little secret—our surprise for the Randville Tigers," Frank said.

One of the faces staring at Frank—the face of Henry Allison—broke into a wide grin. Scott Butler's face remained as serious as ever.

In the moment of pause in the dressing room, the sounds of the Aldridge High pep band could be heard from the field.

"We've got a new wide receiver," Frank said.

Frank could not help glancing at Lenny Parker. Frank's statement was sure to hit Lenny, the starting wide receiver, like a splash of cold water. Frank had considered bringing Lenny into the secret, to ease the jolt. But he could not be sure Lenny would keep the secret. Out of resentment or embarrassment, Lenny might tell. He might even quit the team. So Lenny had to find out he would be sharing his playing time, same as most players learned it—from the coach's announcement.

Lenny frowned, more in puzzlement than anything else, it seemed. Some of the players glanced around as if expecting to find a new face they had missed earlier. Some looked at Lenny.

"Tonight, we'll be passing—to the surprise of the Randville Tigers," Frank said. He stepped across and opened the dressing room door. He stuck his head out.

She was there, in uniform, a helmet dangling in her right hand, a couple of yards down the empty corridor from the door.

"Come in, Jill."

Frank stepped back and Jill appeared in the doorway. She stopped a moment, just standing there, framed in the doorway, and gave a small smile of nervousness. Then she stepped in and took a seat on the end of the bench.

The room was deathly quiet.

Frank had expected the players to be surprised.

A girl? A girl playing football?

All around the room, mouths fell open and eyes widened. Nobody said a word. The players were more than surprised. They were stunned.

Frank gave them a moment to recover, then moved to break the silence. "Jill is an outstanding athlete, as you all know," he said.

Still nothing but stunned silence.

Frank went on in a calm, conversational tone. He described Jill's role. She was to be a sideline receiver and an end zone receiver, to avoid being tackled. She was going to be valuable as a decoy, once the fact of her pass-catching abilities was established.

"Scott and Henry and I have been working secretly with Jill on pass patterns in the evenings—in the gymnasium—for two weeks," Frank said.

Frank glanced around the room, trying to read the players' reactions in their faces. He couldn't. Then he nodded to Scott.

Scott got to his feet and took a couple of steps toward the center of the floor. He said simply, "Believe me, she can catch passes."

Everyone was looking at Jill. She smiled and seemed to shrug slightly.

"All right, let's get out there and win a game," Frank said, and sent the players out of the dressing room.

The Panthers surged down the corridor and out the door opening onto a patch of grass between the field house and the stadium—forty-one boys and one girl, heading for the playing field.

In the swirl of bodies wearing the red uniforms with white trim at the Aldridge High sideline, nothing seemed unusual.

The player wearing number 89 was tall enough to fit into the picture and, with shoulder pads, seemed brawny enough. Jill's helmet partly hid her face, and her short hair did not extend below the helmet.

There was no indication that anyone in the grandstands or on the sideline across the field noticed anything out of the ordinary about the crowd of Aldridge High players.

The pep band was blaring away. In the grandstands people were settling back into their seats after standing to cheer the entry of the stream of Panthers onto the playing field.

Scott Butler and Georgie Francis, as co-captains, marched to the center of the field and won the toss—a good omen, Frank figured. They chose to receive the opening kickoff.

As Scott and Georgie walked back to the sideline, Frank turned and looked up at the press box. Up there, high above the grandstand, the secret was out. Frank had waited until the last minute to send up his starting lineup for the public address announcer.

By now, Frank knew, Alvin Stebbins, the history teacher who had manned the public address system at Aldridge High games for more years than anyone could remember, was gawking down on the field with the new-found knowledge that one of the Panthers was Jill Winston, a girl.

Boots Sheridan, who always sat next to Alvin Stebbins, surely was gawking, too.

Then Alvin Stebbins' familiar voice filled the stadium. "The Panthers' starting lineup on offense," he intoned.

He began with the left end—Eddie McMahon—as tradition dictated. And he progressed through the positions. A huge cheer from the crowd followed the pronouncement of Eddie's name and each of those that came after—until he said, "At wide receiver . . ."

Mr. Stebbins stopped, perhaps still unable to believe the name before his eyes, perhaps fearful he was the target of a practical joke.

Finally, he said it—"Jill Winston."

From the crowd came the start of a cheer—the automatic reaction—and then a sort of collective "Huh?" as the name registered in the minds of the Aldridge High fans.

Frank was watching Jill. She stood still as a statue, her face expressionless. Suddenly Elaine Carter's face appeared in Frank's mind. He wondered if she was up there in the crowd. Probably. What would she do? Then he saw in his mind Edson Smalley's face, always expressive, now registering shock, somewhere up there in the crowd.

Frank turned and glanced across the field at the Randville bench. He located Coach Wilson Nutting in the crowd of players wearing gold uniforms with green trim. Nutting was paying no attention to the loudspeaker announcement. Everything appeared normal at the Randville bench. Apparently Jill Winston's name meant nothing to Wilson Nutting, and nobody was connecting the name to a girl. Maybe Wilson Nutting thought the name was Gil, if he heard the announcement at all.

Mr. Stebbins' final announcement—"At quarterback, Scott Butler"—was lost in the hubbub and shouts and chatter and whistling from the crowd.

Clearly the Aldridge High fans knew Jill Winston.

The kickoff teams took to the field with the Panthers' Marty Elmore deep to receive the game's opening kick and the other players arrayed in front of him.

Involuntarily Frank glanced around, half expecting to see an enraged Elaine Carter coming over the four-foot chainlink fence after him. But she wasn't there to be seen. Not yet, at least.

Frank looked again at Jill, still unmoving, expressionless.

The kick was in the air. Marty, at the fifteen-yard line, his face pointed skyward, moved forward a couple of steps, then to his left, and gathered in the ball. He tucked the ball away and raced straight ahead, up the middle, toward a crowd of Aldridge High blockers trying to blast open a lane for him.

The Randville defenders caught him on the thirty-eight-yard line and threw him to the ground.

Scott Butler led the offense unit onto the field.

Frank noticed that Jill, jogging onto the field, was wiping her palms on her thighs.

Well, Jill Winston wasn't the first football player to have sweaty palms going into a game for the first time.

CHAPTER

7

Jill lined up at wide receiver, alone, to the right, standing easily. Nobody, including the Randville defensive back watching her, seemed to have recognized number 89 as a girl.

Scott moved up to the center, scanned the Randville defense for a moment, then leaned into the center and began barking the signals for the first play—a plunge into the line by Richie Fields.

Scott took the snap, stepped back, turned, and handed the ball to the charging Richie Fields. Richie took the ball in both hands at the stomach, lowered his head, and threw himself into the middle of the line.

Jill loped forward and cut to the sideline. The defensive back watched her come, backpedaled briefly, and then—with Richie's plunge into the line obviously for real—let number 89 go unbothered and unwatched. In the middle of the line, Richie fought his way to a four-yard gain.

Jill and the other Panthers jogged back toward the huddle.

Frank took a deep breath, turned and paced a few steps, then walked back and stared at the huddle—a semicircle of players facing Scott Butler.

So far, so good. The Randville Tigers, in the course of just one play, had revealed their conviction that the Aldridge High Panthers could not—or would not—pass. The linebackers had played up close, jumping into the line at the snap. Even the defensive back facing Jill had seemed almost casual in tracking her.

And now, with no rush of a new player taking the field from the bench with urgent instructions for the Randville defense, Frank knew the Tigers had not recognized Jill Winston as something new—and perhaps menacing—in the Aldridge High attack.

They had not recognized Jill as a girl, either, which Frank considered to be interesting and amusing, but not important. The important thing right now was that they had not spotted the something new on the field for the Aldridge High Panthers.

Well, they were going to notice it now.

Scott broke the huddle and the players lined up. The Randville defense got into position—the linemen shifting, then settling, then shifting again, and the linebackers bobbing around, threatening a blitz.

Jill took up her position to the right. The defensive back facing her wore on his face the first signs something was strange. Maybe he was remembering that number 89 was not one of the numbers whose wearer's abilities had been described to him by his coaches. This was not Lenny Parker. Or maybe he was thinking that number 89 looked sort of like a girl.

Scott did not give Jill so much as a glance when he lined up behind the center and began calling the signals.

At the snap Jill ran forward.

Frank, on the sideline, was counting the steps with her—two, three . . .

Scott faked a pitchout to the left to Marty Elmore, hoping to lean the defense away from Jill on the right, and then took a casual step backward, the ball on his hip.

Frank kept counting Jill's steps—six, seven . . .

The linebackers, recovering from the fake to Marty, were clawing their way through the line. The defensive back was backpedaling, watching Jill. Unlike the last time, he seemed to be sensing something might happen in his territory.

Jill lowered her left shoulder and turned slightly in a fake to the left—a beautiful fake, perfected in years of practice on a basketball court. The defensive back took the bait. He committed himself to Jill's left.

Jill cut to the right, toward the sideline. Scott brought the ball up and fired it at a spot on the sideline.

Jill reached the sideline, stopped, turned, put her hands up—*ker-plunk!*

She looked around. She was alone at the sideline with the ball in her hands. The defensive back was screeching on the brakes, turning, trying to recover. There was nothing between Jill and the goal except empty space and, off to the side, an off-balance and distant defensive back.

For a horrifying second, Frank thought Jill was going to make a run for it. The terrible vision of a tackler catching her from behind and slamming her to the ground as she raced for the goal flashed before his eyes.

"Don't!" he shouted.

Jill took a couple of steps down the field, almost walking, and then stepped out of bounds. She was smiling when she tossed the ball to the referee and jogged toward the huddle.

The play gained twelve yards, carrying the Panthers across the fifty-yard line into Randville territory with a first down on the forty-six-yard line.

The roar from the Aldridge High crowd, mixed with the blaring of the pep band, was deafening. True, it was only one play, only one pass, but the Panthers were moving the ball against the Randville Tigers.

On the next play, Jill again ran straight ahead—same pattern—and Scott, after faking to Richie Fields into the middle of the line, turned toward Jill, brought the ball up, pumped once, and then pitched out to Marty Elmore going the other way.

The threat of the pass stopped the linebackers in mid-play.

Marty, with a half-step head start, gained eight yards around left end to the Randville thirty-eight-yard line before a confused Randville defense recovered and dragged him down.

The cheers from the crowd were even louder, and the

players along the Aldridge High sideline added their own shouts.

But Frank was not cheering. He knew the game was only beginning. The pass to Jill had caught the Tigers by surprise, and it gained twelve yards. The threat of another pass—with the evidence already in that the receiver might hang on to the ball—had enabled Marty to break loose for eight yards on the other side of the field.

But the secret was out now. There was a new and unknown receiver on the field for the Aldridge High Panthers. The surprise was gone. The Randville Tigers were sure to make adjustments. Right now, for sure, the coaches across the field were making their decisions and issuing their instructions. The game had a long way to go to the end. There were tougher tests to come.

Frank stared across the field and saw the Randville head coach, Wilson Nutting, speaking into the ear of a player and then sending him onto the field.

Frank called out, "Scott!" When Scott turned, Frank nodded toward the substitute. Scott nodded his understanding that the substitute was bringing in a change of plans to meet the challenge of the surprise pass receiver.

Still, it seemed, none of them knew that Jill was a girl.

Frank grinned to himself at the thought. He figured he would know the instant that Wilson Nutting discovered the truth. The Randville coach was sure to object. And when Wilson Nutting objected, rockets went off in all directions.

Scott gained three yards on a keeper around left end for a first down on the Randville thirty-five-yard line.

Then he pitched out to Marty, going around left end again, as if trying to turn the Randville defenders' attention in that direction, to help them forget number 89 running patterns on the right side. Marty gained five yards.

Frank caught Scott's eye on the way to the huddle and made a chopping motion with his right hand. Time to give Randville another look at Jill.

The play was the same as Jill's first pass. Seven steps straight ahead, a fake to the left—again, beautiful—and a cut to the right.

Scott faked to Richie into the line, took a step with the ball on his hip, then cocked and fired into the space at the sideline.

Ball and Jill arrived together.

Jill threw up her hands, caught the ball, and stepped out of bounds at the nineteen-yard line, with the recovering defensive back in her wake.

Jill turned to toss the ball to the referee. She was face-to-face with the trailing defensive back.

Frank saw the defensive back's face—a wide-eyed expression of sudden realization—and saw his mouth begin working. Frank could not hear the defensive back's words, but he could imagine them.

Jill grinned and ran around him, shoveling the ball to the referee.

The defensive back ran toward the center of the field, shouting something at a Randville player. The player, presumably the defensive captain, ran to meet him, listened, looked puzzled, then nodded his understanding.

Jill was back at the huddle.

The Randville player turned from the defensive back and stared at the Panthers' huddle for a moment. Then he called time out and jogged to the Randville sideline.

Scott left the huddle and trotted toward Frank. "Jill says he spotted her for a girl," he said.

"It's okay. From the start the only question was when." Frank kept his eyes beyond Scott, focusing on the Randville captain and Wilson Nutting across the field. But he kept talking to Scott. "Now, we're on the nineteen with a first down, and—"

Frank stopped in mid-sentence.

Scott turned to see what Frank was looking at.

Wilson Nutting was coming onto the field, toward the referee. He was shouting something and waving an arm. The referee charged toward Nutting and shooed him back to the sideline. Nutting retreated, still shouting, and the referee followed him, listening.

The referee looked at the Aldridge High huddle. Then he looked across the field at Frank on the sideline. He put his hands up as if trying to silence Nutting, nodded, and started jogging across the field toward Frank.

Frank waited, with Scott at his side. Frank felt a powerful urge to grin—a wide, silly, leering grin. He was feeling immense satisfaction. His judgment of Jill's abilities had been accurate. His idea was working. His team was moving down the field. But he did not grin. He stood and waited.

"Coach Nutting says his players think that your number 89 is a girl," the referee said.

"Yes," Frank said. "That's correct. A girl."

"A girl?"

"That's what I said, yes."

"But you can't—"

"Why not?"

The referee frowned. He glanced toward the huddle, then at Wilson Nutting stomping around at the sideline across the field. He turned back to Frank. "But girls don't play football," he said, apparently at a loss for anything else to say.

"This one does," Frank said. "You've seen her catch two passes."

"But—"

"There is no rule against girls on a football team. I've checked. But I'm sure you already know that."

The referee, still frowning, pursed his lips tightly. Then he said, "Coach Gardner, I hope you realize the responsibility . . . the possibility of—"

"I do realize the possibility, and I do accept the responsibility," Frank said evenly. "For her, and for the boys on the team, too."

The referee stood a moment without speaking. Then he said, "All right," and jogged back across the field.

Frank watched Wilson Nutting wave his arms and work his mouth in front of the referee.

Then the referee returned. "Coach Nutting wants it made clear to you that his players will treat her the same as any other player in a football game. They will not make allowances for the fact she is a girl. And anything that happens is your responsibility for putting her on the field."

"Fair enough," Frank said.

The referee left.

Frank turned to Scott and said, "Tell her to be careful, not to take any crazy chances." Then he sent Scott back to the huddle.

By this time a sprinkling of boos for the referee was starting up in the crowd as the Aldridge High fans realized what all the conferring was about.

The boos changed to a loud cheer when Scott returned to the huddle and Jill stayed in the game.

The Aldridge High fans, it seemed, liked the idea of their Jill Winston catching passes against the Randville Tigers.

Frank, as an afterthought, signaled Scott to throw a short sideline pass to Jill on the next play. Might as well let Wilson Nutting and the Randville Tigers know that Frank and his Panthers, Jill included, were not going to be intimidated.

The play called for Jill to angle to her left, as if heading for a pass over center, then reverse her field and race for the sideline.

With the snap, Jill moved out straight ahead for three steps, then swerved to her left. The defensive back, uncertain, moved with her cautiously. A linebacker hung back, then began moving toward Jill, menacingly, to help the defensive back.

Scott, with the ball, spun and began working his way down the line, giving Jill time to run her pattern.

Jill suddenly reversed herself, with the gracefulness of a dancer, and broke into a headlong run for the sideline.

Scott stopped, straightened, cocked his arm, and threw the ball.

The defensive back and the linebacker both were chasing Jill.

Frank had seen sturdy boys quake at the sound of the thundering footbeats of defenders determined to knock somebody to the ground. But Jill seemed unmindful. She ran, looking back for the ball.

The timing was off a split second—but enough. Jill was a half second late in arriving. Or the ball was a half second early. She got a hand on the bullet pass—but that was all.

The rifling ball zipped across her fingertips and fell to the ground as she ran across the sideline stripe.

Out of bounds she slowed to a halt.

Behind her, the charging linebacker tried to put on the brakes, then tried to swerve. He succeeded in neither and bumped Jill hard with a shoulder.

Jill staggered but kept her feet.

Frank leaped forward to protest. Intentional or not, the jolting shot was a foul.

The referee did not wait for Frank's protest. Without hesitation he called an unnecessary roughing penalty and began marching off yardage to the Randville four-yard line.

Frank sent Lenny into the game for Jill and motioned for her to join him on the sideline.

While Richie Fields crashed through the line behind Henry Allison for a touchdown, Jill was telling Frank, "I've been bumped harder than that on a basketball court."

CHAPTER

8

By halftime the Panthers were leading the Randville Tigers, 14–0.

The locker room, though, was a quiet and somber place, filled with serious faces. While the players seemed to sense they were on the brink of accomplishing the impossible—a victory over powerful Randville just one week after almost falling to tiny Johnson City—they realized that the second half remained to be played.

Frank walked among the players, patting a shoulder, speaking a word of encouragement, offering advice for the plays to come.

On offense, Jill Winston had been the difference between success and failure. She caught four more passes after the two in the drive for the first touchdown. She missed one that she should have caught, but not because her hands failed her. She tried to go around the defensive back blocking her way instead of cutting in front of him. As a result, she was nowhere near the whistling pass that Scott fired right on target. It was a result of inexperience, and understandable, although her face flushed with embarrassment when she realized her mistake.

All in all an outstanding first half for Jill—six of eight passes caught for a total gain of fifty-one yards.

Those six passes for fifty-one yards, plus the simple threat of her running the patterns, provided the aerial punch the Panthers needed to balance their attack.

She led the Randville defenders on a merry chase even when cutting across the center or running a deep pattern. Someday an opponent would realize that Frank had no intention of Jill receiving passes in an open field. But so far Randville's defenders had not noticed. Or if they suspected the truth, they weren't willing to gamble on it.

Marty and Richie and Scott all were finding themselves the happy recipients of a half-step advantage in running plays because the Randville defense had to guard against a pass.

The Panthers' defense was playing brilliantly—an accomplishment made easier by an offense capable of moving the ball. First the opening touchdown gave the defense crew a lift. They took the field with a lead to protect. But also, throughout the first half, the strong offense invariably turned the ball over to Randville deep in Tigers' territory, giving the defense players space to operate, never with their backs to the wall.

Frank knew that there was nothing like a strong offense to make a defense look good. And nothing like a strong defense to make an offense look good. It was one of those bits of evidence that football was, indeed, a team sport.

He glanced at his watch, walked across to the door and opened it, and gestured to the waiting Jill to enter. He closed the door as she took a seat on a bench.

Frank moved to the center of the floor and began ticking off the positive aspects of the first half—everything that had gone right for the Panthers—and said, "You're going to win if you play the same way in the second half. It's as simple as that."

He glanced around at the unsmiling faces looking up at him. There had been some negative aspects to the first half, to be sure. But Frank had, as always, dealt with those on an individual basis. There was nothing to be gained by embarrassing a player in front of his teammates.

"I don't know what the Tigers may try to do in the second half," he said. "But you can bet it will be something different. Something new on offense, for sure, because they obviously need to score. So be alert. Don't assume that what you see developing is going to come at you the same way it did in the first half. They'll be showing us something new. Remember that."

He turned to Scott, and spoke to the offense unit. "There are no real surprises now. They've seen our surprise—and suffered from it. They've spent most of this halftime intermission changing their defense. They weren't expecting passes from us at the start. But they're expecting passes now, and they'll be ready. The yards are going to be tougher to get. So we have to concentrate and make no mistakes. No mistakes."

Scott nodded.

Frank sent them out of the dressing room and down the corridor, headed for the field and the second half.

The clock in the center of the scoreboard showed twelve seconds remaining in the game. The score in lights read: "Panthers 21, Opponents 7."

On the field the Panthers were in possession of the ball on their own forty-one-yard line, and Scott was dropping to the ground with the ball in both hands—the last play of the game.

All around the stadium, the Aldridge High fans took up the countdown: ". . . ten . . . nine . . . eight . . ."

At the sideline Frank shoved his way frantically through the jubilant crowd of shouting, cheering Panthers, seeking Jill.

He found her.

"When we get inside, go straight to my office," he said. "Stay there. I'll come get you. Give me ten minutes or so, and I'll come get you. There's going to be a crowd in the corridor. We'll have to shove our way through. You wait for me, okay?"

The crowd was roaring: ". . . three . . . two . . ."

Jill nodded her understanding.

The buzzer sounded, ending the game. There was a huge cheer from the crowd and from the players in front of the Panthers' bench.

Frank dashed to the center of the field and shook hands quickly with an icy and unspeaking Wilson Nutting, and returned to his players.

"Let's go," he shouted, and they turned and headed off the field toward the patch of grass leading to the field house, by now having to joust their way through crowds of students and fans coming over the short chainlink fence.

Frank, jogging with the players toward the door, sought Jill in the sea of red uniforms. He found her just ahead of him. Players were pounding her on the back in congratulation, and she was giving them shots to the shoulder in return, and laughing.

Inside, Frank stopped at the dressing room door and watched Jill walk down the corridor, still empty, until she disappeared safely into his office. He then stepped into the dressing room after the last player, closed the door, and locked it.

He stood a minute, hands in pockets, and watched the happy players. The shouts and cheers bouncing off the walls of the locker room were deafening and, to Frank, beautiful. So different from the morguelike atmosphere of the dressing room after the Johnson City game.

Towels were flying through the air, from one laughing player to another. A few of the players were already peeling off their jerseys and unhitching their shoulder pads.

Frank stepped into the center of the floor and raised his hands for silence. He turned slowly, and finally something resembling silence fell over the room.

"I want to remind you—especially those of you starting to undress—that one of your teammates—a girl—isn't here—but will be in a moment."

There was laughter from all sides, and somebody shouted, "Jill, Jill, Jill."

"I'm going to get her now," Frank said.

He stepped into the corridor. Already several students and a few adults were there—familiar faces, but nobody Frank knew. He smiled and nodded as he walked through their shouts of congratulation to his office. He knocked at the door, then opened it.

Jill was seated on Frank's desk, her feet dangling a couple of inches above the floor, her helmet on the desk beside her.

"Let's go, Jill."

She came off the desk, the helmet in her hand, and walked past him through the door into the corridor.

At the sight of her approaching them, some in the crowd in the corridor began shouting, and then others joined in.

Frank put his hands on Jill's shoulders in front of him and steered her through the crowd, avoiding meeting anyone's eyes—Elaine Carter's? Edson Smalley's?—until they reached the locker room door. He opened the door and guided Jill through and closed the door quickly behind them. Towels were still flying and the noise had reached a deafening pitch again.

Jill looked around with an expression of wonder on her face, and smiled. Frank realized that she was seeing a winning football team's locker room for the first time—and, at that, surely was one of the few girls ever to do so.

Then the towels stopped flying and the shouting stopped. Suddenly there was a strange silence, with all eyes on Jill and Frank near the door.

Jill, still smiling, gave a short little nod, seeming to say, "We did it," and as if on signal the roaring noise of the cheers erupted again.

Jill stood, unmoving, for a moment, and then sat on a nearby bench.

Frank stepped to the center of the floor. The noise began to die down. Frank waited. Then, with a grin on his face and his arms spread wide, he said, "Enjoy it." And another cheer broke out.

When the players quieted down again, he said in a serious tone, "Enjoy it—and remember it. Remember this game every Friday night of this season. Remember this game in each and every one of our next eight games. This game is worth remembering. It wasn't a miracle, you know, our victory out there tonight. Not a miracle at all. This was a bunch of good football players, playing good football and defeating a good team. It was no miracle. Remember that — you beat 'em. It wasn't a miracle."

Frank stepped back and let the players resume their shouting, having intentionally avoided any mention of the girl who caught eleven of sixteen passes for one hundred one yards.

He opened the door a crack and, as he had expected, found himself face-to-face with Palmer Winston. Frank asked, "Do you want her to change here—in my office—or do you want to take her home?"

"Is she all right? That was a hard jolt she took. You promised me—"

"She's fine. Not hurt at all. She told me that she's taken harder jolts from girls on the basketball court. No problem, really."

Palmer Winston watched Frank for a moment. Then he said, "We'll take her home to shower and change. Tell Henry to pick her up at home for the party."

"Sure."

Frank closed the door and walked over to Jill, now surrounded, and leaned in and spoke in her ear.

She nodded to Frank, then laughed back at the boys for a couple more minutes, and left.

The dressing room was quiet and almost empty. Frank watched the last of the players, Eddie McMahon and Richie Fields, leave. Then Ron left, saying, "See you tomorrow."

Standing alone, Frank took a deep breath and said aloud to the empty room, "Now for the tough part."

He walked to the door, put his hand on the knob, paused a moment, and then opened the door and stepped into the corridor. The students and fans all had gone—friends and parents of the players leaving with them.

Frank saw Carol down the corridor, waiting. With her,

waiting, were Edson Smalley and Elaine Carter. Frank decided to take another deep breath, then approached them.

Edson Smalley was wearing a small smile, a smile that seemed half amusement, half apprehension. Elaine Carter was not wearing a smile of any sort. Her mouth was a tight, straight line. Her eyes were firing rockets.

"I think we'd better talk in my office in the morning, Frank," Mr. Smalley said.

"Yes."

"I'll be there," Elaine Carter snapped.

"Yes."

Frank turned to Carol and then, on impulse, turned back. "We beat 'em," he said with a grin.

Edson Smalley, still wearing the small smile, nodded his head.

Elaine Carter, not smiling, did not nod her head.

CHAPTER 9

Frank drove slowly through a drizzling rain toward the school. His windshield wipers made the only sound. The sidewalks were empty except for the occasional person wrapped in a raincoat, face hidden by an umbrella held low. The streets were almost empty of cars, too, at this early hour on a Saturday morning. The time was eight o'clock.

With his early start, Frank hoped to watch the tape of at least the first half of the game before Edson Smalley— and, yes, Elaine Carter—arrived at the school, requiring his presence in a meeting. There were a lot of notes to be taken, a lot of lessons to be learned from the tape. Down to the finest detail, what were the adjustments that Randville had made in the face of the unexpected threat of Jill Winston? Which of the adjustments had worked and which had not, and why? What might Frank devise to defeat those adjustments against future opponents?

And what might be changed—improved—in Jill's role? Future opponents were sure to study the tapes of the Panthers' games. They were going to be looking for weaknesses to be exploited, tiny errors offering opportunities. They were going to find ways to make Jill's job tougher, less successful. Frank had to come up with new moves to make Jill's job easier, more successful.

Beyond Jill's pass receiving, there were questions to be answered about the Panthers' running game. Helped by having a pass receiver offering a real threat for the first time, Frank was seeing Marty and Richie and Scott run the ball in a truly balanced attack. What worked? What didn't? And why?

A lot of the answers were on the tape. Frank was eager to get at the business of running and rerunning the tape and finding the answers.

As Frank drove through the drizzling rain, this morning's headline in the *Aldridge Morning Herald* kept flashing through his mind: "Jill Winston Leads Panthers Over Randville."

And the overline, in smaller type: "Yes, Jill Winston."

Boots Sheridan's story had been a straightforward account of the game—the runs, the passes, the punts—laced throughout with phrases of understandable astonishment that a girl—a girl!—was catching passes for the Panthers.

His lead paragraph told the story: "The Aldridge High Panthers unveiled a surprise passing attack last night in the form of Jill Winston, a receiver recruited from the girls' basketball team, and registered a stunning 21–7 upset victory over the Randville Tigers."

The story contained not the first hint of Boots Sheridan's opinion of the Panthers playing a girl at wide receiver.

Maybe Boots had been too surprised to make a judgment under the pressure of his morning paper's deadline. Maybe in his eyes the startling victory overwhelmed any personal feelings about a female invading the male game of football. Or maybe he was waiting to talk to Frank . . . and to Edson Smalley . . . and Elaine Carter.

Frank found himself not caring what the sports editor might say when they met later in the morning, and not caring what Boots wrote for the Sunday paper. The players approved of Jill. The fans approved of Jill. And Frank approved of Jill. What did Boots Sheridan matter?

But Frank felt a frown crease his forehead when he saw in his mind again the headline: "Jill Winston Leads Panthers Over Randville." And: "Yes, Jill Winston."

Jill's name was in the headline twice.

And Jill's name popped up time and again in the story.

Jill Winston, the star of the game, was the star of the newspaper story. Not Scott Butler. Not Richie Fields. Not Georgie Francis. Just Jill Winston.

Frank hoped that Scott, who threw the passes that Jill caught, would understand. He hoped that Richie, who scored two touchdowns, would understand. And he hoped that Georgie, and all the others on defense who had bottled up the Randville attack time and again, would understand. And yes, Henry Allison, whose blocks cleared lanes for the runners. Would Henry understand his girlfriend taking over the spotlight? On this day and in the days to come, the black ink in the *Morning Herald* might spell trouble for the Panthers, no matter Boots Sheridan's opinions.

Frank thought briefly that Jill herself might have some problems. In basketball, Jill had been in the hero's spotlight before. But this was different. She was a girl playing a boys' sport. No, more than that. She was a girl starring in a boys' sport.

As Frank passed the tennis courts covered with puddles and the rain continued to splatter down, his frown faded and he almost smiled. At least he didn't have to worry on this rainy Saturday about his secret weapon spraining an ankle playing tennis. Nor, he added to himself unconsciously, his right tackle.

Frank turned into the empty staff parking lot and pulled into a slot near the door. He got out and ran to the door and entered.

Frank shook the few drops of rainwater off his windbreaker and draped it over the back of his desk chair. Before sitting down, he reached for a clipboard on the wall beside his desk.

Then he sat down and scanned the roster list until he came to the name he wanted—Lenny Parker—and moved his finger across to the home telephone number—555-5501. He picked up the telephone and dialed.

Given his preference, Frank would have spoken with

Lenny before he left the dressing room the night before. But there had been no chance. So now the first order of business was to talk with the wide receiver who had lost his starting assignment to—of all people—a girl.

Lenny's father answered.

"Mr. Parker, Coach Gardner. Could I speak to Lenny?"

"Yes. Yes, of course." He sounded pleased that Frank was calling.

Lenny came on the line. "Yes, Coach."

"Lenny, I hope you will support what I am doing."

There was a moment of silence. Then Lenny said, "Well, she can catch passes, that's for sure."

"That's precisely the point, Lenny. Jill Winston has a great deal of a very specialized skill. The team needs that specialized skill. I hope you will understand and support what we're doing."

There was another moment of silence. This time Frank broke the silence. "You're still going to see a lot of playing time, Lenny. The team needs you as much as it needs Jill, but in different kinds of situations."

Frank waited.

Then, "I understand. It's okay. It's just that, well, it came as, you know, kind of a shock there just before we took the field."

"I know it came as a shock, and that's why I'm calling you now. But it had to be kept a secret until the last minute. I hope you can see why."

"Yes, I can." Then a pause. "Now I can see it."

"Okay?"

"Okay. See you Monday."

Frank smiled into the telephone. "Right. See you Monday."

Frank hung up the telephone slowly and his smile faded away. He knew full well the pain and embarrassment his decision had caused Lenny. He hoped the telephone call helped. He hoped the telephone call gave Lenny an answer to any questions around town. Maybe . . .

Then Frank went into the training room, found the tape awaiting him, and began loading the machine for the opening kickoff.

The telephone rang. Yes, Frank could come to the principal's office.

"I think the only question that needs answering already has been answered," Frank said. "And that is, what does Jill want to do? I asked Jill if she wanted to come out for football. She said yes. So what else is there?"

Frank was seated on the end of the sofa across from Edson Smalley's desk. Mr. Smalley was seated behind his desk. As always, he shifted around constantly, trying to use up some of the excess energy that powered him at full speed all of the time. He smiled, frowned, then smiled. He leaned back; he leaned forward. Such fidgeting by a nervous man might be irritating. But Edson Smalley was not a nervous man. And the sparks given off by his energy did not irritate.

Elaine Carter was seated to Frank's left in an overstuffed chair that matched the sofa. Her mouth was a tight line and her eyes were flashing with anger. She was neither tall nor muscular, and Frank figured she must have won her way in basketball by having a deadly shooting eye and a brain—and a fierce competitive spirit.

"Yes," Elaine snapped, "there is another question to be answered."

Mr. Smalley turned from Frank to Elaine and leaned forward, a perfect picture of a man anxiously awaiting the next statement.

"And that," Elaine said, "is—what is best for Jill?"

Mr. Smalley, with a questioning look, turned back to Frank.

Frank shrugged slightly. "It's sort of the same thing, isn't it? It's for Jill to say—and Jill's parents."

"I heard about that," Elaine said.

"Heard about what?" Frank asked.

"The way you got their permission."

Frank looked at Mr. Smalley. The principal was waiting. Frank looked back at Elaine. "I asked for their permission and got it, Elaine—that's all," he said.

"You never mentioned this to me," Elaine said.

Frank was waiting for the statement. "Jill is not your property, Elaine. Jill is a free person. Jill, with her parents, can make up her own mind. You have nothing to say about what other sports—or any other activity, for that matter—she might take part in. That's for Jill to decide, not you."

"Now, now," Mr. Smalley said. He lifted a hand in a conciliatory gesture. "Let's not drift away from the subject at hand."

"Excuse me, Mr. Smalley," Elaine said, "but this indeed is part of the subject at hand. Jill Winston is an outstanding basketball player. She has a wonderful future in basketball. She can go to college on basketball." Elaine stopped and fired a sharp glance at Frank. "I trust you don't envision her as a college football prospect," she said. Then, without waiting for an answer, she turned back to Mr. Smalley. "This football venture that Frank has lured her into threatens her basketball future. For one thing, she could be injured. I saw her take a terrible shot out of bounds last night. For another thing, is she going to miss the start of basketball season because she's playing football? These are important questions for Jill Winston."

"Ummm," Mr. Smalley said, leaning back and looking at Frank as if to ask, "Well, what have you got to say to that?"

"Elaine, you know very well the answers to every one of those questions," Frank said. The words came out with a sharper edge than he had intended.

"Ummm," Mr. Smalley said again, causing both Frank and Elaine to look at him. "But Frank, I think Elaine would like to hear your answers. And so would I."

"Yes, all right." He paused. "First—and most important—she is in no more danger of injury on the football field than on a basketball court. Her role on the team is very narrowly defined, and intentionally so, to reduce the danger of injury as close to zero as possible. As for the jolt she took on the sideline, she told me herself that she had been hit harder on the basketball court."

"All right," Elaine said, "go on."

Frank watched her for a moment. She seemed poised to pounce, patiently waiting for his first misstep.

Mr. Smalley nodded slightly.

Frank plunged ahead. "Elaine, it simply is not true that showing up a couple of weeks late for the start of basketball practice is going to endanger Jill's future basketball career."

Elaine leaned forward. "It's more than a couple of weeks," she snapped.

"May I continue?"

"Please do," Mr. Smalley said.

"Boys play football and then turn out for basketball—and sometimes with great success. Richie Fields did it last year and was named to the all-conference basketball team."

"We will play our first two games before the football season ends," Elaine said.

Frank felt a flash of anger. "So you're afraid you'll lose a game or two without Jill," he said.

"And you're afraid you'll lose football games without her."

Mr. Smalley waved a hand. "Whoa, just a minute," he said.

Elaine turned to the principal. "Mr. Smalley, you told me when you hired me that girls' sports were as important as boys' sports at Aldridge High. But now what we've got is a boys' team's coach raiding a girls' team—and apparently getting away with it."

Mr. Smalley tilted his head slightly, as if weighing Elaine's statement. He looked at Frank and said, "Frank?"

Frank glanced at Elaine's angry face and then directed his remarks to Mr. Smalley. "These are two different sports—football and basketball. Elaine makes it sound like the boys' basketball coach is raiding the girls' basketball team. That's not what has happened. I asked Jill if she would like to participate in a second sport, as many students at Aldridge High do every year." He glanced at Elaine. "It's not a question of boys' sports or girls' sports being the more important." He turned back to Mr. Smalley. "It's a question simply of what Jill wants to do."

"Uh-huh," Mr. Smalley murmured.

Elaine sat without speaking, watching the principal.

"Frank," Mr. Smalley finally said, "you really should have consulted me on this. There is more involved than just Jill Winston . . . just the football team . . . or"—he glanced at Elaine—"just the girls' basketball team. Do you understand what I mean?"

Frank shifted uneasily. He had known the question would be coming, and he dreaded it. Yes, he should have consulted the principal. But he hadn't. How was he to explain it?

"I knew there would be a flap when the word got out, and we didn't need a flap in advance," Frank said. "Something might have popped up in the midst of a flap to keep Jill from playing."

"I'll say," Elaine interjected.

Mr. Smalley shook his head at Elaine.

"Also," Frank continued, "I did not want to tip our hand to the Randville coaches that we had a pass receiver."

The reminder of the victory over the Randville Tigers brought a small smile and an expression of pleasant remembrance to Mr. Smalley's face. He did like to see his Aldridge High teams win.

"Mr. Smalley, what are you going to do?" Elaine demanded.

The smile and the expression of pleasant memories disappeared, to be replaced by a lifting of the eyebrows. "Do?" he asked.

"Yes. What exactly are you going to do?"

"Nothing, Elaine, nothing."

In the long moment of silence that followed, Frank kept his gaze focused on a corner of Mr. Smalley's desk. He was pleased by the principal's refusal to intervene. He knew that Elaine was angrily displeased. He did not want to give her the slightest basis for saying he looked triumphant.

Elaine broke the silence. "I assume," she said, and Frank looked across at her, "that there is no objection if *I* do something." She was looking at Mr. Smalley.

Mr. Smalley gave a small, gentle smile. "Anything short of harassment will be permissible," he said.

Frank returned to his office to find a waiting Boots Sheridan.

"Well, the gimmick worked," the sportswriter said for openers. "I'll have to hand you that."

The tone of voice implied that Frank had pulled some sort of trick—something unfair, unethical, even if technically legal—to defeat Randville. The statement also seemed to him to imply that the trick, once used, lost all its value. Jill Winston, having arrived on the scene and performed her function, now would vanish as quickly as she had appeared. The Panthers, having cashed in on a stunt, now found themselves again—or still—without a passing attack.

Boots' expression showed that he could hardly wait to ask the obvious question: What are you going to do now?

Frank stared at Boots. Then he said, "It wasn't a gimmick."

The full meaning of Frank's statement took a few seconds to register with Boots. Then his face showed genuine surprise. "Do you mean that you intend to continue playing Jill?" he asked.

"I sure do."

"You can't be serious."

"Why not? She's fully eligible, a bona fide student of Aldridge High, and she's a superb pass receiver. You saw that for yourself."

Boots took in the statement and seemed to be turning it over in his mind. Then he said, "She's a good athlete, and I'll admit she's sturdy—but she's a girl, and they'll break her in two."

Frank grinned slightly. "I've heard that before. Several times, as a matter of fact." He leaned forward. "But they did not break her in two in the Randville game, and they won't do it in any game." He paused a moment and then said, "Boots, it should be obvious to you and all the rest of the world that we're not going to throw to Jill in a dangerous situation."

"It just"—Boots hesitated and frowned—"doesn't seem right."

"C'mon, Boots, face it, we're headed for the twenty-first century. The girl can catch passes better than anyone else walking the corridors of Aldridge High. She wants to play. Is it right to tell her she can't just because she's a girl?"

Boots didn't answer the question. Instead he asked, "What does Elaine Carter have to say about this?"

"You'll have to ask her."

"And Edson Smalley?"

"You'll have to ask him."

Boots nodded and jotted something in his notebook and, without looking up, asked, "Can I interview Jill?"

"You know that I don't allow interviews with my players."

"This is different."

"Different only in that the no—*no*—is louder."

Boots glanced up, seemed on the verge of saying something, then had a change of mind and nodded his acceptance of the rejection. "Okay. Tell me from the beginning, will you, how this came about?"

"Sure."

Frank leaned back and started talking. He began with a girls' basketball game on the evening of February 14. He ended with Jill entering the dressing room before the game.

The hour was almost three o'clock and the rain was still drizzling down when Frank drove home from the school, pulled into the driveway, got out, and jogged along the flagstone walkway and entered his house.

He had spent almost an hour with Boots Sheridan, detailing the sequence of events that led up to Jill Winston taking the field and catching passes against the Randville Tigers. Frank had chosen his words carefully. He left out Henry Allison completely. He made the initial interview with Palmer Winston sound like a simple conversation from the beginning, instead of the explosion that it really was. He said nothing of the meeting with Edson Smalley and Elaine Carter. He emphasized Jill's natural abilities and the two weeks of hard work with Scott Butler in the gymnasium.

Boots scribbled notes, seldom breaking into Frank's narrative with a question.

"You realize," Boots said at the finish, "that the wire services are probably already picking up on this. You're going to get a lot of attention."

Frank shrugged. "I guess," was all he said.

Then, finally, Boots left, and Frank turned his attention at last to the game tapes.

He spent more than three hours viewing the tapes—Jill Winston surprising an opponent with her first catch, Jill Winston playing against an opponent no longer surprised, Scott Butler passing and running, Marty dancing around the ends, Richie plunging into the line, Henry blocking, Georgie Francis sparking the defense.

Frank covered four sheets of legal-sized yellow paper with penciled notes.

As Frank was leaving, Ron Matthews entered, surprised to find Frank still there. Their normal practice was to view the tape separately—Frank in the morning, the assistant coach in the afternoon—and then compare notes. That way neither one of them affected the other's impressions during the viewing.

Frank explained briefly the reasons for his lateness and departed, leaving Ron watching the opening kickoff.

"You've got a dozen phone messages," Carol said. "Everyone from the North-Central Conference headquarters to the AP. Do you want a sandwich first?"

"Uh-huh," he said. Then a thought struck him. "I've got a couple of calls of my own to make first," he said.

He carried the telephone to the sofa and dialed Scott Butler's number.

"Everything okay?" he asked the quarterback.

"Great," Scott said. Then, "Is anything wrong?"

"Not a thing. Great here, too. Just wanted to check."

A puzzled Scott said, "Okay."

Then Frank dialed Jill Winston's number.

"You okay?" he asked.

"Sure."

"Got any bruises?"

"A bit of one, but no problem. I've had bruises before."

"Okay?"

"Yeah, why?"

"Just checking."

Frank hung up the telephone and sat a moment without moving. He knew why he had called them. Everything could not possibly be so perfect as it seemed. Jill caught passes and the Panthers beat the Randville Tigers. Mr. Smalley didn't object to Jill playing football. Elaine Carter's complaints to Mr. Smalley got nowhere. Elaine was going to keep trying—she had said as much—but that was fair enough. Scott Butler was happy. Jill Winston was happy. Even Lenny Parker seemed okay.

And it was even raining, which probably explained why he was able to reach Scott and Jill home so easily on a Saturday afternoon.

Everything could not possibly be so perfect.

CHAPTER

The rest of the weekend flew by for Frank. He spent Saturday afternoon and early evening returning telephone calls and answering the ringing telephone.

The sportswriters—from Chicago, St. Louis, Indianapolis, all the big cities of the Midwest—had read on the AP wire about the girl pass receiver at Aldridge High in Illinois, and they were calling her coach to develop stories of their own.

They all asked the same questions. Was the idea Frank's or Jill's? Was Frank worried about injury to Jill? Was Jill worried about injury? What did her parents think? Where did a girl named Jill Winston learn how to catch a football? What did the boys on the team think about having a girl teammate?

And always: How about an interview with the girl?

Frank answered their questions carefully. He offered

little more than the straight answers he had to give. He rejected all requests for an interview with Jill or any of the other players. And then he went on to the next caller.

Three of his telephone calls did not involve sportswriters.

Nolan Coleman, the principal of Fisher High in neighboring Broadview Heights and the president of the North-Central Conference, called with dire warnings of trouble, if not disaster, unless Frank regained his senses and dropped Jill from the football team.

"As president of the conference, I feel a responsibility," he said. The principals of the eight schools of the North-Central Conference rotated the presidency of the conference. They usually passed their terms serenely, presiding over meetings with no problems on the agenda. Nolan Coleman clearly bemoaned the fact that fate had put him at the helm in the year that Aldridge High fielded a girl at wide receiver. "It is up to me, as president of the conference," he said, "to ensure that all sports schedules are played out in the proper spirit, and with the safety and development of the players always the top priority."

Frank, listening, raised an eyebrow. He never had met Nolan Coleman. He wondered if the Fisher High principal always spoke in such stilted terms. Maybe Coleman was reading from a carefully drafted statement. That was what it sounded like.

Frank's first inclination was to cut off the conversation with a suggestion that Coleman call Edson Smalley if he felt that Aldridge High was giving the conference a problem. After all, Smalley was not only the principal of Aldridge High but also a member of Coleman's conference board. Then the thought occurred to Frank that Nolan Coleman possibly had already called Edson Smalley, and the result had been a zero, politely delivered. Edson Smalley was fully capable of telling Nolan Coleman: "Frank Gardner is the football coach, and it's his decision, as long as no rules are broken."

So Frank responded to Coleman by saying, "I don't think that you, as president of the conference, need feel any responsibility at all, if we're within the rules, and we are."

"Have you considered the possibility of injury to the girl?"

"Of course. I always consider the possibility of injury to any and all of my players," Frank said. "That's my responsibility, and Aldridge High's responsibility—in the case of Jill Winston and also in the case of every other member of the team—and not the responsibility of the conference."

In the pause that followed, Frank heard Coleman take a deep breath. Then Coleman plunged ahead. "The other schools in the conference are concerned," he said.

Frank nodded unconsciously. Coleman was getting to the real reason behind the call. Somebody was protesting—maybe several somebodies—and trying to put pressure on Coleman. Perhaps Randville High was protesting. The Tigers were frustrated and angry losers because of the passes Jill had caught. Or teams yet to come up on the schedule, teams that would prefer not to cope with defending against a girl, particularly a girl who could catch passes. Frank said only, "Oh?"

"I've already had calls from two schools," Coleman said.

"Well, so?"

"What shall I tell them?"

Frank spoke curtly. "Tell them that there's no conference rule against a girl playing for the Aldridge High football team. It's that simple."

Coleman said nothing for a moment.

Frank waited without speaking.

Then Coleman sighed into the telephone, as if trying to convey regret that Frank was forcing him into saying what was coming next. "If you persist in this," he said, speaking the words slowly and distinctly, "I cannot predict what action the conference board might take."

Frank grinned into the telephone and shook his head. Again Coleman sounded as if he was reading from a prepared statement. The veiled threat of board action—declaring Jill ineligible, perhaps ordering the forfeit of victories in which Jill took part—struck Frank as empty and laughable. He said only, "I understand."

"You're being very negative about this whole thing."

"I think I'm being very positive."

Coleman again said nothing for a moment. Then he said, "Thank you," and hung up.

Frank replaced the telephone in its cradle but kept his hand on it a moment, considering briefly whether he should call Edson Smalley. Then he decided against it.

If he hadn't already heard from Nolan Coleman, the principal was sure to hear in the next few minutes. Either way, Edson Smalley did not need Frank's advice.

The other two callers, both women, were not so easily handled.

One spoke at length about Frank's courageous act in the interests of advancing equal opportunities for women.

"I want you to know," she said, "that your courage is no less than that of Jill Winston."

Frank listened, first in surprise, then with a tinge of embarrassment, as the woman rambled on. Frank considered himself a football coach, not a crusader. He was more interested in a wide receiver catching passes than women's rights.

Finally the woman quit and hung up.

The other caller berated Frank. Only a male chauvinist of the lowest order would stoop to exploiting a young girl's talents in his own drive for success in a game played by animals.

Frank blinked at the assault. At one point he started to ask if the woman considered him also to be an exploiter of the talents of boys. But he opted for silence, hoping that was the quickest way to end the call.

After the second woman's call, Frank dialed Jill. "Are you receiving any funny telephone calls?" he asked.

"Some sportswriters," she said. "One from Chicago," she added, obviously impressed.

"Oh?" For a moment Frank was alarmed.

"I didn't talk to them. Coach Carter always said the players couldn't give interviews, and I figured it's probably the same with you."

"Yes, right," Frank said. "Anything else?"

Jill laughed. "A couple of women. They were funny."

"Funny?" Frank asked, but he was sure he knew what she was talking about.

"Yeah. One of them thought I was a hero. The other one thought I was a victim."

"Uh-huh. What did you tell them?"

"I told them both that they were wrong," she said with a laugh.

Frank grinned. "Okay," he said.

He was about to hang up when Jill, with the tone of an afterthought, said, "Oh, Coach Carter came by this afternoon."

Frank's grin faded. "Coach Carter," he said, and waited.

"She doesn't think I should be playing football."

Frank rolled his eyes and credited Jill with the understatement of the year. Then, with an uneasy feeling in his stomach, he asked, "What happened?"

"Well, nothing. She just talked."

Frank had no difficulty imagining what Elaine Carter might have had to say. But he asked, "What did she say?"

"Well, she told us—"

"Us?"

"Me. My mother. My father."

"I see. Go on."

"She said there was a chance that I might be injured,

that I was endangering my senior year of basketball, that I needed to think of my future—you know, all those sorts of things,"

"Uh-huh," Frank said and waited.

"I explained about the patterns—just sidelines and all that—so I won't get tackled."

"Ummm."

"She said nobody could guarantee that I wouldn't get hurt."

"What did your father and mother say?"

"Mother didn't say much. She thinks this is a kind of neat idea, you know."

Frank thought, yes, but Palmer Winston did not think it a neat idea for his daughter to play football. "And your father—?"

"Dad seemed to get a little miffed. You know," she said, "he doesn't like for people to tell him what he should do. He told Coach Carter that we had all decided that it would be all right for me to give it a try for a while, and that was that, and he didn't want people—he meant her—tugging at me."

Frank's right eyebrow went up half a notch. Palmer Winston did not much like the idea of his daughter catching passes on the football field. But it seemed he liked even less listening to advice from Elaine Carter. There was a good chance that the basketball coach had inadvertently bolstered Jill's chances of continuing her football adventure.

"And you?" Frank asked.

"Me?"

"Yes." Frank was sure he knew the answer. It was obvious that Elaine Carter had failed to convince Jill and her parents to reverse their decision. But she might have raised some doubts, regrets, worries in Jill's mind. If so, Frank wanted to know about them. He did not want Jill playing football out of a sense of misplaced commitment or, perhaps, plain stubbornness; he wanted her to play out of a desire to play. Her easy-going ways revealed little of her true feelings. So he asked the question, "Did anything of what Coach Carter said raise any doubts in your mind about what you're doing?"

"She talked a lot about injuries. But I'm not worried about that. I've been knocked down in basketball games. I can take care of myself."

"Anything else?"

This time Jill hesitated before answering. "She doesn't want me to miss any basketball practices. She says it will hurt my playing in my senior season and will hurt the team."

Frank waited to see if she had anything more to say. He could hear Elaine, with her clipped words, driving her points home. When Jill did not speak, Frank said, "Well, you're not missing any basketball practices yet."

"That's what I told her."

Again Frank waited.

"I told her that I was doing this because I wanted to, and that it wasn't interfering with basketball, and that I'd have to make up my mind what to do when the time came."

Frank nodded slightly to himself. Elaine Carter had

failed, but not without scoring some points. But Jill had given Frank the words he wanted to hear. His smile returned. "See you at practice," he said.

"Right."

On Sunday morning, Frank read Boots Sheridan's story in the *Aldridge Morning Herald* with great care. He was sure the story was being read with great care in other quarters, too—in the Winston household, at Edson Smalley's breakfast table, in Elaine Carter's house, and certainly in the homes and offices of the football coaches in neighboring school districts.

A quotation, from Elaine Carter, brought a flicker of a smile to Frank's face: "No comment. I'm the girls' basketball coach. I don't have anything to do with the boys' football team. I have no comment." Frank could hear Elaine snapping the words out.

Boots' story, in sum, was fair and accurate. He gave a chronological account, from the first appearance of the idea in Frank's mind to the moment Jill caught her first pass. He dealt with the injury aspect—the fact of a girl playing in a rough game always reserved for boys—by quoting Frank directly: "We have designed pass patterns that minimize the danger of injury."

The appearance of the quote pleased Frank. He had made the statement to Boots—not once, but several times—in the hope of seeing it in print. He wanted to reassure, once again, Mr. and Mrs. Winston, Edson Smalley, and yes, even Elaine Carter. As for opposing coaches reading the true meaning in the statement,

Frank figured it would take a pretty dumb coach not to already recognize the limits of Jill's role.

In the afternoon Frank went to his office at the school. Ron was already there, prepared for their regular Sunday afternoon meeting to compare notes on the last game and chart the practice week leading up to the next game.

The next opponent on the Panthers' schedule was the Hutchinson High Wildcats. The Wildcats were a team with one victory and one loss in the young season—a team with the Panthers' old problem: no passing attack.

Frank, with a grin, asked Ron, "Do you suppose the Hutchinson coaches are working right now with a girl from their basketball team in an effort to solve their passing problem?"

Ron grinned back and shrugged. "Maybe so," he said. "It's not a bad idea."

"If the Wildcats put a girl on the field, I think we should file a protest," Frank said.

"Of course," Ron replied.

They both laughed.

There seemed to be a lot to laugh and smile about around the Aldridge High football office, all of a sudden.

Then came Monday.

CHAPTER

11

The television crews—three of them, two from up in Chicago and one from down in Champaign—arrived at the practice field almost simultaneously, ten minutes after Jill and the other players took the field.

"Which one is she?" somebody called out. "They all look alike."

The players were formed up in three rows at the end of the field, going through a series of loosening-up calisthenics. In their practice uniforms, they did not offer even jersey numbers as a helpful guide to identification by strangers.

"There she is—third row," somebody else called out.

The three television crews, as one, began moving across the practice field.

Frank, carrying the clipboard containing the practice

plan, turned and marched away from the rows of players, toward the advancing crowd.

"Get off the field," Frank barked, waving the clipboard at them.

There were eight of them, seven men and one young woman. The woman, wearing jeans, a sweatshirt, and sneakers, carried a camera on her shoulder. Two of the men carried cameras. The crowd kept coming.

"Off, off," Frank repeated, waving the clipboard again as he continued his approach.

The crowd slowed, hesitated, then stopped to await Frank's arrival. As he walked up to them, one of the men stepped forward and said, "Coach Gardner, Sandy Meadows, Channel Four."

Frank had seen the smiling, handsome face on his television screen at home.

"You'll have to get off the field," Frank said. "We're starting practice."

"Coach, all we need is a little footage of the girl—Jill—catching a few passes. Won't take but a minute."

"No."

"What?"

"No. I said, *no*."

Behind them Frank saw other strangers approaching. There were a half dozen of them. Some had cameras dangling on straps around their necks. It appeared that the out-of-town newspaper reporters and photographers were arriving right behind the television crews.

Frank took a deep breath and tried to shift his mind

into high gear. He had not anticipated this onslaught. Sure there had been the Saturday morning interview with Boots. That was standard, and he had known the conversation would be all about Jill Winston. Even the later telephone calls from sportswriters had not been unexpected. After all, a girl catching passes on a football field was not an ordinary everyday sight.

But a mob of television crews and out-of-town sportswriters swarming onto the field in the opening minutes of practice? Not for a moment had the possibility entered Frank's mind.

He searched through the crowd for the familiar face of Boots Sheridan. Being one of them, maybe Boots could explain why Frank was not going to have his practice session interrupted. But Frank knew he would not find Boots' face. The *Morning Herald* reporter invariably arrived midway through practice, then stayed to the finish. Boots had no need to watch the warming-up calisthenics and the preliminary work that led to the serious business of the session.

But Frank had to do something.

Before he could speak, the young woman with the video camera on her shoulder piped up. "He can't stop us from shooting on the sideline," she said. "With this little baby"—she patted her video camera—"I can bring her in. It's okay."

Frank turned from Sandy Meadows to the young woman. "Yes, I can stop you from shooting from the sideline," he said. "This is school property. You are neither faculty nor staff nor students. Without permission you have no business here. I can have you removed, and I'll do it if you interfere with my practice session."

The newspaper reporters and photographers joined the crowd—a semicircle of more than a dozen people in front of Frank.

"Aw, now, Coach," Sandy Meadows said.

"He's bluffing," the young woman with the video camera said.

Frank looked at the young woman for a moment without speaking.

Sandy turned to her. "Christy, for Pete's sake, turn it off, will you? Just shut up for a minute."

Frank started to turn, to call out for Ron to go inside and summon Josh Abbott, the Aldridge High security man. Frank had no intention of wasting another minute of his practice time with them. Josh, for all his gentle manner, had handled some tough cases. He would have no trouble ushering a dozen reporters and photographers off the school grounds.

But Frank stopped when one of the late arrivals, apparently a newspaper reporter, said, "Coach, excuse me, but maybe we could stay and just watch practice, and then when practice is over, maybe—if it's okay with you and Jill—we could take a couple of pictures of Jill and talk to you for a few minutes." The man was smiling pleasantly. "We understand that you don't want your practice disrupted."

Frank nodded. "That'll be all right with me," he said. "But now, if you please, off the field."

He turned and, without looking back, walked to the three rows of players still bending and twisting in their warm-up calisthenics—all faces turned toward the confrontation up the field.

"Hold 'em up a minute," Frank said to Ron, and Ron brought the players to a halt. Frank spoke in a conversational tone that carried to both ends of the three lines of players. "Those are television and newspaper people. They're going to stay and watch our practice. They will not bother us. And you will pay no attention to them."

Frank waited a minute to let the words sink in, then walked to Jill and said, "They want to take some pictures of you after practice. I have no objection, if you don't."

"Is that Sandy Meadows of Channel Four?" Jill asked.

"Good grief," Frank muttered under his breath. Then aloud he said, "I assume that means you have no objection."

For the television crews and the newspaper reporters and photographers sprawled on the grass alongside the practice field the Aldridge High Panthers' drill was a disappointment. They were there to see Jill Winston, girl pass receiver, in action. But what they saw during the practice session were boys—Marty Elmore, Richie Fields, Scott Butler—running.

The Panthers, finally with a passing threat to ease the pressure on the ball carriers, spent the afternoon honing their running attack. The run, not the pass, always was the heart and essence of an offense devised by Frank Gardner.

In the early going Frank glanced across at the group several times and was satisfied to see the woman named Christy seated on the ground, hugging her knees, her video camera resting idly on the ground next to her. Later he noticed the approach of Boots Sheridan, moving toward the group and then joining them, shaking hands with several of the reporters and crew.

At the finish Scott and Jill remained on the practice field after the other players had trooped to the dressing room. For fifteen minutes Scott drilled his bullet passes to Jill while the photographers, bobbing and shifting around, recorded the action on tape and film.

Then for another fifteen minutes, after Scott and Jill had left, Frank sat cross-legged on the ground with them and answered their questions, with Boots watching silently from the edge of the group.

There were no new questions. Frank had heard them all before, either from Boots or from the sportswriters calling on the telephone. And there were no new answers. They could have gotten the same information by reading Boots' story in the Sunday paper.

The week rolled on toward the Friday night date with the Wildcats at Hutchinson.

Jill was the star of the sports segment on the ten o'clock news in Chicago and Champaign on Monday night, and on the six o'clock news on Tuesday evening. Her face appeared in photographs in the Chicago, Champaign, and Peoria papers on Tuesday morning. To Frank's relief, the camera crews and the reporters did not return.

Boots Sheridan stood at the sideline of the practice field each day and watched, then wrote his account of the day's drill for the readers of the *Aldridge Morning Herald*. Frank was gratified to see that Boots, in print, treated Jill as just another of the players working toward perfecting the execution of the game plan developed to defeat the Hutchinson Wildcats. Even on Wednesday, when Frank sent Scott and Jill and a center to one side to work for almost an hour on a new set of pass patterns, Boots wrote only that the Panthers devoted time to their passing attack.

But Frank decided to take no chances on Boots Sheridan, nor on the increasingly large crowds that turned up to watch practice, when the time came to introduce Jill to the receiving end of a long bomb pass thrown by Scott.

The sight surely was a strange one for any students who happened to glance out classroom windows on the south side of the building during the third period. Frank, with the promise that he would ask only this one time, obtained Jill's release from her study hall and Scott's from his American history class to join him on the practice field.

And there, for more than thirty minutes, Scott, in street clothes except for cleated football shoes, and Jill in her usual jeans and blouse but with cleated shoes, worked on forty-yard pass plays. Time and again, Scott took the ball from Frank and backpedaled. Jill flew down the field toward the goal. Scott wound up and threw the ball as far as he could. Jill looked over her shoulder, veered her route slightly, adjusted her speed, and gathered in the ball.

At the finish Frank nodded his approval. Jill, in a sprint, was even faster than Frank had thought. The Panthers had a startling new weapon in their arsenal.

As the week moved on, the players seemed to Frank to be accepting Jill as a teammate. They all, to the last one, seemed to have discarded their first flashes of disbelief—and perhaps doubt—probably in the seconds after she caught her first pass against Randville. Now everyone, even Lenny Parker, seemed to accept her. If there were any resentments or jealousies, they did not show, and Frank was willing to settle for that.

To Frank's knowledge, Elaine Carter did not reappear, either at the Winston household or in Edson Smalley's office. Frank, busy with the planning and the practice of midweek days in football season, did not see her at all.

During the week, Frank did not hear from Palmer Winston—and, for sure, Palmer Winston did not hear from Frank. In the lack of contact, the agreement that Jill could play remained in place. Any conversation could mean only problems.

By Friday morning Frank was thinking only of the Hutchinson Wildcats. Everything else—the difficult job of persuading Palmer Winston, the secret sessions in the gymnasium, the hassle with Wilson Nutting and the referee in the Randville game, the final victory over Randville, the meeting with Elaine Carter in Edson Smalley's office, the conversation with Nolan Coleman, the episode with the television crews and the sportswriters—all seemed far behind, far, far back in the past.

All that mattered now was the Hutchinson Wildcats.

The pep band blared away unseen from the orchestra pit in front of the stage in the Aldridge High auditorium.

Across the front of the stage, eight cheerleaders in white skirts and sweaters trimmed in red swayed and clapped their hands to the music. Behind them the Aldridge High Panthers were strung out across the stage, some grinning nervously, others staring without expression across the rows of students in the seats.

Above the stage hung a giant banner, white with red lettering, that echoed in three words the astounding triumph over Randville the week before: "Now for Hutchinson."

Off to the side, standing at a podium, Frank waited for the end of the music to introduce a half dozen or so of the players who had distinguished themselves in the previous game.

Frank spotted Edson Smalley standing at the rear of the auditorium, arms folded over his chest, a huge smile on his face. And Frank saw Elaine Carter standing at the side. She was not smiling.

The music faded away and the cheerleaders skipped off the stage, four to each side.

Frank leaned down toward the microphone and began ticking off the names of the players. First, Georgie Francis. Frank always began with a defensive player. The stocky nose guard stepped forward, grinned, and waved, and everyone cheered. Then Richie Fields, Marty El-more, Scott Butler, Henry Allison.

Then Jill Winston.

A long cheer rocked the auditorium.

Frank did not declare that Jill Winston was a girl. Instead he said, "The receiver of eleven passes for a total of one hundred one yards."

Jill, grinning, took one step forward. Frank looked back at her while the cheering resumed. Jill did not wave. She nodded slightly, acknowledging the cheers, continuing to grin. Then she took one step back into her place in the line.

At the finish the students poured out of the rear doors of the auditorium and the players and cheerleaders left by a stage door to board the school buses for the fifty-mile ride to Hutchinson.

CHAPTER

12

By the moment of the game's opening kickoff—the ball high up there in the darkness, flickering its reflection of the arc-lights, tumbling end over end, with Marty Elmore looking up at it from the fifteen-yard line—Frank was distracted, angry, and worried.

The ball now dropping toward Marty's waiting hands seemed a million miles away. The roaring cheer of the standing crowd in the grandstands on both sides of the field seemed a distant echo. The Aldridge players on the field in their visiting-team uniforms of white trimmed in red seemed nothing more than a blur.

Standing on the sideline, Frank frowned deeply and tried consciously to jerk himself back from the problems of the last two hours and into the concentration needed for the beginning of play.

The trouble had started when the buses carrying the

team arrived at Hutchinson High, a sprawling modernistic building of glass and steel, a few minutes before six o'clock. The highway trip, interrupted by a prearranged break at a truck stop for sandwiches, had taken almost two hours.

A man wearing khaki trousers and shirt, and a blue cap with an orange "H" emblazoned on the front, was waiting for the buses in front of the school building. He got up from his seat on the steps in front of the school and waved the buses into a driveway that led between the building and the stadium. He jogged to the front of the first bus and led the way to the back of the building, then pointed them toward parking slots.

When Frank stepped off the bus, the man approached and said, "This way," and walked toward double doors leading into the building. Frank followed the man, with the players streaming off the buses behind Frank and the man.

The man opened the double doors, led the way inside, stopped at a door, then opened it, and said, "Visitors' dressing room."

Frank nodded.

Around them players moved into the dressing room and two student managers began lugging the Panthers' gear—uniforms, pads, shoes, helmets—from the bus into the dressing room.

"We've got a girl on our team," Frank said. "Where can she dress?"

The man shook his head dumbly.

Frank waited.

Then the man grinned in a silly way. "I don't know nothin' about a girl," he said. "You mean, you've got a girl on your football team?"

Frank felt the first twinge of anger. The man was joking, surely. If he didn't know there was a girl on the Aldridge High football team, he had to be the only person within a hundred miles who was ignorant of the fact. Frank's anger increased. He was sure the man was playing with him. "Yes, we have a girl who is a member of our football team," Frank said coldly.

The man shrugged, still grinning. "I don't know," he said.

Frank glared at the man. Part of his anger began to turn inward, on himself. Probably he should have called Hutchinson High during the week. He should have made sure the Panthers' special need was known. Stupidly he had assumed that dressing space for Jill—an office, or a girls' washroom—would be no problem. Well, it was too late now.

Finally Frank asked, "Is Coach Hanson around?"

"Naw, not yet. He'll get here about six-thirty when the Wildcats start arriving."

"All right," Frank said. He turned and walked outside and approached Jill near the door. "Get back on the bus and just relax for a few minutes," he said. "I'll come back for you."

"Is something wrong?"

"Nobody who's here now seems to know where you're supposed to dress out," Frank told her. "We'll get it worked out."

Jill stepped onto the bus and took a seat in the front row and Frank walked inside, past the man in khaki, and into the dressing room.

Thirty minutes later, with the Panthers beginning to move out for their limbering-up exercises, Frank set out in search of the Hutchinson High coach. The man in khaki was nowhere to be seen, but the corridor, empty when the Panthers had arrived, now had a stream of boys moving through it.

Frank stopped one of the boys. "Can you point me to Coach Hanson's office?" he asked.

The boy gestured toward a door at the end of the corridor and said, "There, inside the dressing room."

Frank thanked him and walked toward the door. Opposing coaches did not normally visit each other's dressing rooms just before a game. But Frank, with mounting anger, had decided that either the man in khaki had not relayed the word of Frank's problem, or Coach Buck Hanson was ignoring it.

Frank pushed his way through the double swinging doors and walked in. Beyond a couple of dozen half-dressed boys at lockers, Frank recognized Buck Hanson sitting on a desk behind a glass wall. He was talking to a younger man, probably an assistant coach, who was standing in front of him with his back to Frank.

Frank and Buck Hanson had met only once, and that briefly—the midfield handshake at the end of last season's game, a 24–0 victory for the Hutchinson Wildcats over the Aldridge Panthers. But there was no mistaking the barrel-chested man with the bull neck and the flattop haircut.

Hanson frowned when he saw Frank, and the young man with him turned to see who was approaching. When Frank stepped through the door into the glass-enclosed office, Buck Hanson greeted him with, "What're you doing in here?"

Frank did not even blink at the gruff question. He knew the type. He had played against them, and he had coached against them. They saw football as war, and the opposing team as the enemy, and they gave away nothing—not even courtesy.

"Coach Hanson," Frank said, offering neither a handshake nor a response to the Hutchinson coach's surly greeting, "where is the girl on our team going to dress out?"

"Anywhere she wants," Hanson said with a laugh and a knowing glance at the younger man.

Frank kept his eyes on Hanson and waited.

"You've found the visitors' dressing room, haven't you?" Hanson asked with another laugh.

"I need a place where she can change into her uniform," Frank said flatly.

"Well, I guess you do."

"Where is a room that she might use?" Frank asked.

Hanson shook his head in mock puzzlement. "I don't really know," he said slowly. "You know, at Hutchinson High, we don't think that football's a sport for girls. We think it's a sport for young men. Never had the problem of where to dress out a girl for a football game."

Frank stood, unmoving, determined to stay there until right through the scheduled moment of the kickoff, if necessary. He resolved that his Panthers would not take the field without Jill, dressed out in uniform and ready.

Frank took a breath and said, "You know, if you've finished with your little joke, you do have an obligation to provide whatever dressing room facilities are needed for the visiting team." He meant the statement as a threat to refuse to play the game without one of his players, but he stopped short of saying it.

Hanson seemed to get the message. "Okay," he said, "c'mon."

Hanson lifted himself off the desk and onto his feet and walked past Frank. He led the way out of the office and through the dressing room. He called out to his players as he went, "This is the coach with a girl on his team."

Some of the players laughed.

In the corridor, walking along, Hanson turned to Frank and said, "My boys play rough, and they're going to treat your girl just like any other player on the field. She may get hurt. That's the way we play football at Hutchinson High—for keeps—and if somebody wants to throw a girl into the game, so be it."

Frank gritted his teeth and nodded without speaking, fearful of what he might say.

"That's not a threat, you understand," Hanson said. "Just a fact."

"Okay," Frank said.

They turned a corner and Hanson gestured at a door. "That's the girls' bathroom. Nobody down here will be using it tonight. You can have it."

Hanson walked away without another word, and Frank stood there alone in the corridor a moment, thinking. Surely no coach would encourage a player to intentionally hurt another one. But Buck Hanson's words, despite his disclaimer, came across clearly as a threat.

Frank remembered how confident he had been of his pass patterns keeping Jill out of harm's way. He remembered he had been able to convince Jill and her parents that there was no danger, even after the late hit out of bounds in the Randville game.

Now, for the first time, doubts about sending Jill Winston into a football game swept over Frank. Could he, with his clever pass patterns, protect her from a player determined to lay a jolting hit on her? Could he guarantee her safety on the field?

He could hold her out of the game. At the start he could say he was holding her out until she was needed. Then, if the Panthers took a lead, he could say there was no need to risk her. Or, if the Panthers were trailing, he could insist that they needed to stick to the running game, not throw passes.

He was the coach. He could tell her anything, and she would have to accept it.

But no, he could not tell Jill any of those things.

To hold Jill out of the game because of a remark by Buck Hanson would put the lie to all his promises about her safety. Were the promises lies? No. And it would put the lie, too, to his belief in Jill's confidence that she could take care of herself. Did he believe in her confidence? Yes.

Then a final question settled the matter in Frank's mind: What if it had been Scott—not Jill—that Buck Hanson mentioned in a threatening way? Would Frank have considered holding Scott out of the game? The answer came quickly and without doubt: No, not for a minute. But Frank would have cautioned Scott, and he would caution Jill.

Frank came out of the field house and walked around the front of the bus. Jill got up, but Frank waved her to a halt and stepped up into the bus. "Just a minute," he said.

They sat, side by side, on the front seat of the bus.

Jill frowned. "Is something wrong?"

"The Hutchinson coach—Buck Hanson—just made a point of telling me that his players were going to treat you just the same as any other player on the field."

"Uh-huh."

Frank paused and watched Jill. She was still frowning slightly. But there was no hint of alarm, or even concern, in her expression. She seemed simply to be waiting for him to continue. He gave her a small smile. "Maybe I'm overly sensitive. After all, Buck Hanson said nothing more threatening than Wilson Nutting had said on the field during the Randville game."

Jill said again, "Uh-huh," and waited. Then she said, "You're going to let my play, aren't you?"

"Yes, I am. But you've got to be very careful. You must remain alert at all times. You must not relax just because the play has ended, or because you're out of bounds. Stay alert."

"Sure," she said.

Frank waited another moment. Then he said, "Okay, let's go."

The ball finally came tumbling down out of the arclights and Marty caught it. He took a step to his left and then veered sharply to his right and shifted into high gear, heading for the sideline where a wall of Aldridge High blockers moved into place.

Henry Allison and Georgie Francis and all the others held off the Hutchinson High tacklers trying to knife through for the necessary seconds, allowing Marty to race into the corridor. Marty, running between the wall of blockers and the sideline, crossed the twenty-five-yard line, the thirty, the thirty-five, the forty.

At the forty-three-yard line, in front of the Aldridge High bench, not ten yards from where Frank stood, a Hutchinson tackler finally broke through and knocked Marty out of bounds.

The Panthers' offense unit, headed by Scott Butler, moved onto the field to take up play at the Panthers' forty-three-yard line.

Frank stepped across to give Marty, now back on his feet, a pat on the back. But Frank wasn't looking at Marty. He was watching the offense unit take the field, searching for number 89. He found her in the crowd of players with their backs to him, moving toward setting up a huddle.

She was not wiping sweaty palms on her thighs this time.

But Frank was.

CHAPTER

A strange sound rolled down from the grandstands and across the field.

It was not the roaring cheer of the hometown Hutchinson High fans on their feet to root for their Wildcats on the first play from scrimmage. It was not the predictable shouts of encouragement, urging the Wildcats' tacklers to throw the Aldridge High Panthers back on the first play of the game. There was no shouting to be heard. The sound more resembled a loud whisper, a murmuring.

Frank had heard the sounds of football crowds most of his life—the silence at the moment before kickoff, the swelling roar that built up in the kick returner's first couple of steps, the groans that followed a fumble, the sudden explosion of noise as a runner broke loose in the secondary, the sharp exclamation—followed by a long "oooooh"—that acknowledged a great tackle.

Frank knew all the sounds so well. He had often thought that he could turn his back on the field and, by listening to the sounds of the crowd, identify what was happening on the field. But this sound—a hushed, muffled rumbling—was something new.

He unconsciously glanced back at the grandstand, seeing nothing to give him a clue to the explanation. Then he looked back at the field. He saw number 89 taking the last couple of steps toward a place in the Aldridge High huddle. He understood then the meaning of the new sound. It had been several thousand voices, all together, saying to someone next to them—"That's her"—"There she is"—"She's number 89, see?"

All eyes were on her, and all voices spoke of her, but she leaned forward in the huddle, hands on her knees, looking for all the world as if this was a role she had played all her life.

After all, Jill had been successful last week against Randville. And against the Tigers she had continued to be successful long after they discovered that, yes, she caught passes with the expertise of a talented veteran.

So why was Frank nervous? What was new tonight?

Frank knew that a lot was new. This time, the defense was ready for her, had prepared for her all week, would be watching her from the first play, had their instructions. He wondered if Jill realized, even after all his warnings, how much was new.

At least one new element, one difference from the

Randville game, did not matter in Jill's case. Against Randville she played on the home field before a crowd of her friends and fellow townspeople. Here she was playing before the opponent's fans, a crowd that wanted to see her stopped, forced into failure. Any athlete felt the difference, but none more than a basketball player—performing so close to the crowd—and Jill had been a basketball player. She was sure to have no trouble playing football for the first time before a hostile crowd.

On the field the Panthers broke the huddle and moved into position for the first play. Scott stepped up behind the center, glanced left and right, then bent his knees slightly, reached in, and began calling the signals. Jill, out wide to the right and standing ready, looked about to break into a huge grin. Her face was serious, but her sparkling eyes had the look of laughter. Jill Winston was having fun.

Frank felt a slight easing of the gnawing worry. A player having fun, confidently and exuberantly performing the tasks of the game, was less vulnerable to injury. It was the unsure player—worried, hesitant, reluctant—who most frequently fell in harm's way.

The Hutchinson High defensive back opposite Jill did not appear about to break into a huge grin. He seemed to know that he was not there to have fun. He clearly viewed the situation with extreme seriousness. He kept his eyes, unblinking, on Jill. Nervously he clenched and unclenched his fists.

His assignment from Coach Buck Hanson was written in the determination on his face: Don't let the girl catch a pass; but if she does catch a pass, hit her before she steps out of bounds, and throw her to the ground. Probably Coach Hanson had even told him, as he had told Frank, "At Hutchinson High, we play for keeps."

Scott took the snap, stepped back, turned, and handed the ball off to Richie Fields charging toward the middle of the line.

Jill broke into a run, straight ahead, and then angled toward the sideline, looking back—but knowing there would be no pass to her on this play. She crossed the sideline out of bounds with her defender dancing alongside her all the way.

Richie tucked the ball into his stomach with both hands, lowered his head, and crashed into the middle of the line. The Hutchinson High line sagged in the face of ferocious blocking. Richie slashed through a narrow gap between two players, ran over an off-balance linebacker, and gained nine yards to the Hutchinson High forty-eight-yard line before being dragged down.

Frank, his arms folded across his chest, nodded his approval. If the Panthers' running game was able to bend and break the Hutchinson High defense, Jill's role could be minimized, confined mostly to decoy.

On the next play Scott gained two yards and a first down on a quarterback sneak. Then, alternating Marty around left end and Richie into the line, the Panthers marched twenty-five yards in five plays to the Wildcats' twenty-one-yard line.

The Hutchinson High fans who came to see a girl catch passes were so far seeing only a girl running pass patterns while ball carriers slashed into the line and zipped around end. The tense defender facing Jill, while diligently chasing her on every play, had yet to face a test.

The Panthers' runners were shredding the Wildcats' defense almost at will, and the stadium was quiet except for the distant and faint cheers of the small crowd of Aldridge High fans across the field.

But the easy yardage on the ground was sure to come to an end.

Frank could see the signs of a shifting—and a tightening—of the Hutchinson High defense. The gainers on the ground were going to be harder to come by. The shredding of the defense by the blockers and runners was going to be tougher.

True, there was no shuttling of Hutchinson High players back and forth, on and off the field, relaying instructions for a revised defense. And there was no time-out called for Coach Buck Hanson to outline changes needed to stop the running attack.

But there were changes—small, subtle differences— in the defense, unconsciously initiated by the players themselves.

As running play followed running play, Frank noticed them. After Marty's second scamper around left end, the Wildcats' defenders seemed almost to be leaning in that direction. It was as if some secret voice had told them that the Panthers did not want to run to the right, where a girl might get caught in a collision. As Richie continued to pound the middle of the line, the Wildcats' linebackers gradually inched in closer and stepped up the reckless-ness of their charge. They were increasingly sure with each play that the odds favored run over pass, and the left over the right.

Jill's defender, though, was not one of those deciding that every play was sure to be a run, sure to go the other way. He acted as if he was sure that every play was going to be a pass to the girl running patterns to the sideline in front of him. With a jerky, dancing motion, he stopped, started, and cut, sticking to her like a shadow every step of every pattern.

But a pass or a run to the right was what the Panthers needed. Either way, Jill would be the key—pass receiver or decoy clearing out the area.

Frank quickly weighed the choices. Then he stepped forward toward the sideline and caught Scott's eye as the quarterback returned to the huddle. Frank lifted his right hand and spread all five fingers. Scott nodded his acknowledgment, as if he had been expecting the signal. Probably Scott, on the field, had felt the gradual shifting of the Hutchinson High defense.

Scott leaned into the huddle, and Frank could see his mouth working. He also saw Jill look up, suddenly more attentive, and then nod her head a couple of times.

Frank made a mental note to warn her about giving out an indication she was a central figure in an upcoming play. A sharp-eyed defender watching from across the line of scrimmage could pick up the signal, interpret it correctly, and doom the play before the huddle had been broken.

More out of habit than genuine concern, Frank glanced at the Hutchinson High defenders. Nobody was waving at anyone. Nobody was calling out to anyone. Apparently Jill's response to the play being called by the quarterback had gone unnoticed on the other side of the line of scrimmage.

In this case, too bad. The play's success depended on everyone watching Jill, perhaps even chasing after her.

Scott broke the huddle and the Panthers lined up. He called the signals, took the snap, and backpedaled quickly.

Jill took off with the snap—four strides straight ahead, and then a sharp veer to the left, angling at full speed through the Hutchinson High secondary into the center of the field, arms outstretched, face turned back, watching for a pass.

Her defender, having tracked her to the sideline on seven straight plays, lost a second in his surprise when she cut to the left, toward the middle of the field. Then he took off after her. Clearly the defender's assignment was Jill Winston, wherever she might go.

Scott, looking to his left at Jill's racing form, cocked his arm for a pass.

The fake stopped in his tracks the linebacker who should have been moving over to fill the gap left by the defensive back chasing Jill. Only for a second. But it was enough.

Scott, turning back to his right, brought down the ball and shoveled it out to Marty, who was making his cut at the sideline. Marty gathered in the ball on the run, pivoted, and turned on the speed into the space left empty by the Wildcats.

The linebacker recovered quickly and, taking advantage of a good angle, caught Marty and shoved him out of bounds at the Hutchinson High nine-yard line.

The linebacker had saved a touchdown, but Marty had gained ten yards and a first down in the shadow of the goal.

Frank shouted at Marty—"Way to go!"—as the speedy back jogged to the huddle. But Frank knew the ten yards had been gained every bit as much by Jill, whose threat cleared out the area, as by the running of Marty.

Three plays later, Richie Fields, running behind the sturdy blocking of Henry Allison, tumbled into the end zone for the touchdown. Scott, backing away and watching after the handoff, leaped into the air and shouted when the referee threw up his hands to signal touchdown.

All along the Aldridge High sideline, players were on their feet, shouting. And from across the field, the cheers of the Aldridge High fans rang out through an otherwise silent grandstand.

At the moment that Richie took the handoff and hit the line, and before Scott shot his fists in the air in exultant celebration of the touchdown, Frank saw a remarkable sight in the end zone.

Beyond the clash of bodies at the line of scrimmage, Jill was running a crossing pattern designed to distract a linebacker's attention, if not lure him, away from Richie's charge into the line. Her designated defender was racing with her across the end zone. Another defensive halfback was moving toward her from the far side.

Jill dipped a shoulder, planted a foot, and faked her pursuer into flat-footed helplessness. The other defensive halfback, approaching her, came to a halt, unsure which way to go. For a few seconds—plenty of time—she was completely open for a pass, with no one within three yards of her.

The movement was a bit of artistry developed on a basketball court. In football it was a bit of artistry sure to spell touchdowns.

Denny Hoyt kicked the extra point, and the Panthers led, 7–0, without having to throw a single pass to Jill against the Wildcats, who, as Buck Hanson had said, played for keeps.

CHAPTER

14

The picture remained in Frank's mind: Jill, dipping a shoulder, planting a foot, so obviously turning to her right, forcing a commitment from first one defensive halfback and then another—and then smoothly reversing herself, cutting to her left, putting herself in the open, and leaving behind a pair of confused and defeated defenders.

Frank could not remember ever seeing a high school receiver execute a fake so perfectly and with such devastating impact. Professional football players all knew how to do it. The college ranks had many players able to do it. Even among high school players, Frank had seen some pretty good ones along the way.

But Jill Winston, with rhythmic coordination and the experience of a thousand fakes on the basketball court, showed more skill running a pattern in the second football game of her life than Frank ever had seen from a high school receiver.

The picture stayed in Frank's mind while the Panthers' defense, buoyed by the one-touchdown lead, stopped the Wildcats cold in their first possession, forcing a punt. And the picture remained when Scott Butler and the offense took the field and began their second march toward the goal.

The Panthers' offense again slashed through the Wildcats with surprising ease. Richie hit the line twice for gains of seven and eight yards. Marty scampered around left end for eleven yards. Jill caught a sideline pass for six yards, eluding her defender with a quick skip out of bounds. Scott picked up nine yards on a cutback keeper to the right while Jill led her defender the other way, toward the sideline.

With a first down on the eight-yard line, Frank walked down the sideline and waved an arm at Scott and then called out to him. When Scott turned, Frank held up his right hand with the five fingers spread and made a chopping motion: Send Jill on a crossfield pattern—in the end zone—and throw the ball to her.

Scott blinked in surprise, briefly frowned, and then nodded his acknowledgment.

Frank understood Scott's puzzlement. The linemen were shoving the Hutchinson defenders all over the field. The runners were shredding the Wildcats. They had driven to one touchdown. Now they were driving to another. They could punch the ball over from the eight-yard line. Why chance a pass?

To his own mild surprise, Frank realized that he considered the play no risk at all. Jill would elude her defender. Scott would throw accurately. And Jill would catch the ball.

Frank nodded back at Scott and stood, his arms folded over his chest, as the quarterback leaned into the huddle and called the play.

Frank, watching, had no doubts at all.

The Panthers broke the huddle and lined up.

The defensive back facing Jill was standing on the goal line, his mouth set in a straight line of determination, his fists clenching and unclenching. Maybe the picture of Jill's end zone fake of a few minutes earlier was flashing in his mind, too.

Jill stood easily, her weight on her left foot, her face showing nothing, as Scott called the signals.

At the snap Jill ran straight forward in a loping kind of stride.

The defensive halfback watched, then backpedaled, keeping his eyes on her.

Scott turned with the ball and held it out to Richie, who plunged into the line as Scott withdrew the ball and turned.

One of the Hutchinson High linebackers took the bait and threw himself into Richie. They both tumbled to the ground, dragging some struggling linemen with them.

Jill crossed the goal line into the end zone, veering her route slightly to the left. The defensive halfback danced slightly as he watched and waited. Was she going to cut right and head for the corner of the end zone? Or turn left and race the width of the end zone? Jill, running easily, gave no indication.

Scott pivoted and moved along the line to his right, first with the ball concealed on his hip, then openly tucked away for a run.

Jill cut to her left and began sprinting through the end zone. The defensive halfback took off after her. The other defensive halfback saw her coming and moved up cautiously, glancing around to make sure another receiver wasn't moving into the end zone space behind him.

Scott was slowing and looking, taking a passer's grip on the ball.

Jill slammed on the brakes. The defensive back behind her raced past, scrambling to try to recover. The defender in front of her approached as she planted her right foot, lowered her left shoulder, and—clearly obvious to the whole world—prepared to cut back to receive a pass.

Scott, now almost stopped, was cocking his arm.

The approaching defensive back, seeing Jill commit herself, plunged forward. The defensive back who had overrun her was turning and coming back after her.

Then Jill shifted her weight from the right foot to the left, spun slightly, and resumed her sprint through the width of the end zone.

She was open.

Scott fired the ball.

Somebody in the Hutchinson High defense shouted, "Pass!"

But it was too late.

The bullet spiral rifled over the line of scrimmage. Jill,

now looking back, plunged forward. The ball was coming in low, with a fraction of a degree too much lead. Jill bent, stretched, and grabbed the ball.

The referee threw his hands in the air, signaling touchdown.

Two defensive backs, immobilized and left behind by Jill's fake, stared at their shoes.

Scott shot a fist in the air and shouted something.

The players along the sideline sent up a cheer.

Jill, slowing, turned with the ball held in both hands. She was smiling. Then she casually tossed the ball to the referee, ducked her head, and trotted toward her cheering teammates at the sideline.

Frank stepped forward and extended a hand.

Jill grinned at him, slapped his hand, and kept going to the bench.

By halftime the score was 21–0 and Frank had long since started flooding the field with substitutes. The second-stringers were far from the match of the likes of Scott and Jill and Marty and Richie, and Henry in the line and Georgie Francis sparking the defense. But they not only held off the Wildcats, but piled on a touchdown of their own.

For all of Coach Buck Hanson's tough talk, his Wildcats were punchless on offense and weak on defense. But Frank was less surprised by the Hutchinson Wildcats' weaknesses than his own Panthers' strengths. With the simple addition of a passing threat, his offense had evolved in less than two games into a powerhouse attack.

And, as always, the defense benefited proportionately.

As the last minute of the first half was ticking off the clock, Frank, on a sudden impulse, sought out Ron Matthews and led him away from the players at the bench. Gesturing to the corner of the opposite grandstand where the Aldridge High fans were seated, he said, "Go across and get one of the cheerleaders to go in with Jill at halftime."

"Do you think—?"

"No, I don't think there's going to be any trouble," Frank said, and he meant it. But he figured there was a lot of difference between sitting alone in Frank's locked office in Jill's own home stadium at Aldridge High and waiting alone in a public girls' rest room. "It's just that she'll probably feel better with company."

Ron nodded. "Okay," he said and headed out around the end zone to the other side of the field as the buzzer sounded, ending the first half.

Frank walked among the players in the dressing room, offering a compliment here, a criticism there, and then left the dressing room to bring in Jill.

He walked down the corridor and knocked on the door of the rest room.

Two voices responded almost simultaneously. Jill's voice said, "Yes?" Another girl's voice said, "Who is it?"

Frank opened the door and the two girls—Jill in uniform, the other girl in the red-and-white sweater and skirt of an Aldridge High cheerleader—came out, Jill carrying her helmet in her hand.

Frank looked at Jill. "Okay?" he asked.

"Sure."

He turned to the other girl. "Thanks very much," he said. He knew her face from the corridors of Aldridge High and from the pep rallies, but not her name.

The cheerleader said, "Uh-huh," and left.

"Something wrong with her?" Frank asked as he and Jill walked back to the dressing room.

Jill gave a small laugh. "Yeah," she said, "Ellen wanted to meet her boyfriend at halftime."

Frank reflected with a smile that his football strategy was now having an impact on a second romance. "I thought you might feel more comfortable having some-one with you," he said.

"I'm okay."

Frank glanced at her. "I believe you," he said, opening the dressing-room door and stepping back to allow Jill to enter.

Frank opened the second half with the Panthers' start-ers back on the field. He watched them score two touch-downs in three possessions, all the while stopping the Wildcats at every turn. Then he began inserting substi-tutes again.

In the end the score was 37–7.

It was Ron, standing near the door, who heard the rapping above the cheering and chattering and laughing in the dressing room. He opened the door a crack, looked out, nodded, and closed the door again. He walked across to Frank. "Mr. Winston is at the door."

Frank frowned. There had been no bumps for Jill in the game, neither out of bounds nor inbounds. Palmer Winston had no reason to be troubled this time. "Does he want to come in?" Frank asked. Frank always made clear to players, parents, and fans that the dressing room was for players only.

"He just said he wants to talk to you."

"Okay." Frank walked to the door, opened it, and found himself staring into a relaxed and smiling face, nothing like the worried and angry expression that Palmer Winston presented after the Randville game—and Jill's jolting bump on the sideline.

"When she's ready," Palmer Winston said, "we'll give her a ride home."

Without thinking, Frank frowned. That was in violation of another firm rule: All players always rode the team bus back to Aldridge High from road games. He almost launched into his oft-delivered explanation of the reasons for the rule. Then he stopped himself, smiled at Palmer Winston, and said, "Sure, fine."

"She can't exactly shower and change here," Palmer Winston said with a smile, nodding toward the sound of forty boys and one girl shouting and laughing beyond Frank.

Frank nodded, "I'll send her out in just a few minutes."

CHAPTER

15

In the next three weeks Frank told himself time and again that the last problem was behind him and his Aldridge High Panthers. True, the Panthers' world appeared a brighter place every day. But things kept popping up.

The three weeks brought three victories—a 28–7 crushing of the Ashville Bears, a 35–14 thrashing of the Fisher High Yellowjackets, a 21–0 shutout of the Clay City Bulldogs.

Here they were, just over halfway through their ten-game season, and the Panthers, undefeated, already had won one game more than the five victories of the previous season.

They were riding atop the North-Central Conference standings, needing only a victory over either the Coal Hill Miners or the Fayette Pioneers to clinch the championship.

Through the three victories Jill Winston rolled on, virtually unstoppable—and, luckily, untouchable. Her natural grace enabled her to weave through defenders quickly and easily, whether taking in a pass or playing the role of decoy—and all of it without collision.

Not since the out-of-bounds jolt in her first game had she received anything more than a glancing bump. She was used to running in heavy traffic on a basketball court. Most of the time, with the patterns drawn by Frank, she was running in lighter traffic on the football field.

She caught passes with a confidence that grew every time Scott Butler sent the ball like a bullet in her direction. She had the hands—the "feel"—of a born pass receiver.

All told, she caught forty-one passes for a total of two hundred fifty-eight yards—and four touchdowns—in her five games.

The other players in the backfield—Scott, Marty, Richie—continued to blossom as the season moved forward. True, they all benefited from the threats posed by Jill Winston's talents. That was as Frank had expected. But their improvement on their own—Marty's quickened speed around the ends, Richie's added power hitting the line, Scott's improved poise—came as a pleasant surprise to Frank.

The sum total of it was that the victories that Frank had hoped to eke out, with a girl pass receiver giving the Panthers a semblance of an aerial attack, had all turned out to be runaway triumphs.

As a sort of fringe benefit for Frank, Lenny Parker had

caught two touchdown passes in the swamping of Fisher High. After three weeks of glum waiting, Lenny found something to laugh and grin about.

However, twice the spotlight of celebrity focused on Jill with enough glare to give Frank reason for concern.

To his surprise, a television crew from Chicago appeared at Ashville to record Jill Winston in game action for a segment on a network weekend-magazine-type show.

Frank wanted to refuse, and he had no difficulty coming up with reasons.

First, his Panthers could not afford to have Jill distracted. A blink of an eye could mean a dropped pass. That reason alone, in Frank's mind, seemed sufficient for rejection. But even before Frank could get that objection out of his mouth, he saw another reason not to like the idea—the expressions on the faces of some of the players watching his conversation with the television crew in the corner of the dressing room.

So far there had been no resentment of the girl pass receiver. Even Lenny, although certainly not happy, was going along. So far there had not been the first sign of jealousy. But now Frank saw, or thought he saw, hints of envy barely beneath the surface on the faces of some of the players watching them.

Further, Frank wanted to refuse for a reason that had been lurking in his mind from the beginning. What if the network television show portrayed Jill as some sort of freak—a female with the brawn and the unfeminine instincts necessary to play the boys' game of football?

The fear had guided Frank's every comment to every interviewer from the start. So far it hadn't happened. But what about now?

In the end Frank had little choice but to accept the presence of the television crew at work during the game. The Ashville High officials had agreed as a matter of course without consulting Frank. It was, after all, their home game in their home stadium. Frank had to accept the fact that the television crew was properly accredited by the host school to cover the game, same as Boots Sheridan and any other reporter.

Jill, for her part, gave them a show. She caught nine passes, one a leaping grab in the end zone for a touchdown.

As it turned out, the television program depicted Jill as simply a girl, a perfectly normal girl except for a remarkable talent for catching passes and, as the announcer put it, "an adventuresome spirit."

Frank watched the program at home with Carol, heaved a sigh of relief at the presentation—and then the next day faced the writer from *Sports Illustrated* magazine sitting in Edson Smalley's office.

Could he interview Jill?

"No," Frank said and explained his policy.

"Now, Frank," Edson Smalley said, smiling.

Frank, gently steered by the principal, finally agreed to give Jill a list of written questions from the writer, and to return to him whatever written answers Jill chose to provide.

Jill, with a wide grin and an exclamation—"Really!

Sports Illustrated!"—took the questions and wrote out her answers, and Frank passed them on.

The writer, tongue in cheek, came out in print the following week with the statement: "Jill Winston may be a girl pass receiver. But I can't say for sure. Her coach would not let me get close enough to ask."

Jill laughed, and so did the other players. Frank rolled his eyes and hoped his contacts with the national media were at an end.

Away from Jill and off the field, the problems all seemed to slide away into nothing as the touchdowns and the victories piled up.

Before the only game away from home requiring a long bus trip—the game at Clay City—Frank picked up the telephone and called the Bulldogs' coach. He did not want a rerun of the scene with Buck Hanson at Hutchinson High. This time he was going to make sure in advance that dressing facilities were available for Jill— and without hassle. If not, she could dress before the bus trip. She would be riding home with her parents after the game anyway.

Frank need not have bothered.

"It's already taken care of," said Adam Brewster. The veteran coach, now nearing retirement after more than thirty years at the helm of Clay City High football, sounded as if he was wearing his usual smile. He added, "My daughter—she's an English teacher at the school— will meet your girl when the buses arrive and make sure she finds the dressing room."

Frank thanked him and marveled at the difference between two high school coaches—Buck Hanson and Adam Brewster.

During the three weeks, the telephone calls to Frank's and Jill's houses—the angry callers and the elated, as well as the sportswriters—tapered off until there were none.

Not even Nolan Coleman called Frank again. Perhaps the president of the North-Central Conference had tried his plaintive pitch on Edson Smalley and gotten nowhere. Frank did not know. Edson Smalley never mentioned Nolan Coleman to Frank, and Frank did not ask.

Palmer Winston's glare of anger and worry at the dressing-room door after the Randville High game was a thing of the past. He no longer frowned. More often he smiled. It seemed that one play in the Hutchinson High game—Jill's cross-field run as a decoy, springing Marty loose down the sideline—convinced him that Frank was being true to his promise to keep Jill out of harm's way.

"My heart leaped into my throat when she cut left and started running across the center of the field," he had recounted to Frank. "You'd promised me that she would be catching sideline passes and end zone passes and wouldn't be tackled. But there she was—running into the thick of things, a perfect target."

His heart returned to it proper place in his chest when he realized she was a decoy—not a pass receiver to be tackled—and his heart never jumped into his throat again. He continued to meet Jill after every game, but his face offered the smile of a proud father instead of the frown of a worried one.

Boots Sheridan continued to refrain from criticism in his column in the *Aldridge Morning Herald*. But the memory of the sports editor's initial reaction remained in Frank's mind. Frank opened the paper each morning with a twinge of apprehension. Was this going to be the day Boots blasted him: Frank Gardner was endangering a girl in a boys' game; Frank Gardner was taking unfair advantage of opponents who might be reluctant to slam a girl to the ground? Frank was sure of Boots' inner feelings. He knew what to expect from him if Jill should somehow be injured. No doubt about that.

Barring injury, maybe the fact that all of Aldridge was cheering the girl who danced her way into the open and snagged passes for the undefeated Panthers was keeping Boots Sheridan from rolling out the heavy artillery and firing away.

Maybe. But Frank still had uneasy thoughts each morning as he turned to the sports pages of the newspaper.

In the corridors of Aldridge High, the excitement of the victories increased with each passing week. The members of the team liked wearing the smiles of winners instead of the glum expressions of losers. Acknowledging shouted congratulations was more fun than explaining what went wrong. The other students talked about "our team," instead of "the Panthers." Frank could not help noting the contrast with the mood—among team members and others alike—at this point in the previous season.

Jill wore her celebrity well, which did not surprise Frank. For two years she had been an outstanding player on the basketball team. The spotlight was nothing new to her. She knew how to handle herself.

As for Henry's fears, only one person teased him about dating a member of the football team—Jill herself.

"I told Henry that dating a member of the football team was fun, and he decided to give it a try," she announced.

Everyone laughed, including Henry, and Frank smiled when he heard about the wisecrack from a teacher at the faculty table in the cafeteria during lunch. Jill, and only Jill, could get away with it with Henry. And if Jill led the joking, what bite was left in anyone else's teasing? Frank chalked up the episode as another bit of evidence that Jill Winston knew how to handle herself.

And what about Elaine Carter these days?

Well, Elaine Carter was quiet. She wasn't smiling. And she wasn't friendly.

But at least she was quiet.

On Monday, the first day of the practice week leading up to the game with the Coal Hill Miners, Frank sensed the electricity of the players the instant they poured onto the field for the warm-up calisthenics.

The sparkle, the sizzle, the unmistakable excitement in the air—these were the invisible but almost tangible elements of a football team ready to win. The Panthers were heading into a game which, with victory, would clinch the North-Central Conference championship.

Frank, trotting onto the practice field behind the players, felt himself being caught up in the excitement. It was a good feeling. There had been no such electricity last season, not once, as the Panthers plodded through their schedule to five victories, five defeats. Frank remembered the horror of the season opener against the Johnson City Trojans, and the dismal slump the following week. The electricity began, he knew, in the early minutes of the Randville game, and it had built up each week.

Now, with the Coal Hill Miners on the horizon, the Panthers seemed to be at the top of their curve. The Panthers were going to need to be at their best. The Miners, beaten once, were still in the championship race, and they were tough—tough enough to defeat the Randville Tigers and send them, with their second loss, falling out of the run for the title.

But watching his players zip through practice, Frank had no doubts they had decided to whip the Miners and win the championship.

Frank turned the key, locking his office door, and walked with Ron Matthews down the short corridor and into the gymnasium, heading to the cafeteria for lunch. The bell signaling the end of the fourth period rang as they emerged from the gym and started up the single flight of stairs to the main floor.

It was Thursday, and the afternoon to come held only

a light signal drill to wind down the preparations for the Coal Hill Miners on Friday night.] The Panthers' preparations were complete—or, if not complete, the hour was too late. Thursday was no day for introducing a new play, a new wrinkle, a new strategy. That sort of work was done on Monday and Tuesday, with polishing on Wednesday.

Frank was satisfied with the preparations. Now only the game's final buzzer could tell whether he was right.

Frank and Ron came out of the stairwell and moved into the corridor, crowded with students headed in the same direction, toward the cafeteria.

Frank spotted Jill standing at the corridor bulletin board outside the administration offices. She was reading something. Then, as the two men approached through the crowded corridor, she turned and walked on. Frank saw her stop outside a classroom door, wait a moment, and then join the emerging Henry Allison and walk on toward the cafeteria.

Curious, Frank angled toward the bulletin board. Then he realized that he knew the words typewritten on the light green sheet of paper before he read them: "Sign-up for the girls' basketball team will be held in the gymnasium on Monday, beginning at 3:30 P.M." It was signed, "Coach Carter."

Heavy black clouds on Friday morning gave Frank ample warning before he got out of bed, and the rain began falling shortly before noon. Frank and Ron hailed two student managers out of a study hall, and all joined the ground crew in laying out tarps over parts of the playing field where experience had taught that the drainage was poor.

The rain was heavy, with huge drops splattering down on the field and the people unfolding the tarps. The dark sky offered no hope of a quick end to the rain.

Frank knew that the rain was sure to favor the Coal Hill Miners. The Coal Hill team made up for a shortage of skill by being simply physical. They were not so talented as strong, and they tailored their attack to take the fullest advantage of their strength. They relied on a burly line with brawny backs blasting through, running over people.

The rain fit the kind of attack the Miners offered.

As for the Panthers in the rain, who knew? Jill Winston had never caught a pass in the rain. She had never tried a sharp cut or a button-hook maneuver on rain-slick grass. She had never veered her path running a pattern on mud beneath a patch of sparse grass. Rainstorms and wet fields were not the stuff of basketball experience.

Frank and Ron looked at each other as they walked back into the school building, both thinking the same thoughts.

"It could be worse—snow," Ron said.

"Yeah," Frank said.

CHAPTER

16

The rain, though slackening, was still falling at game time, and the field was soggy with occasional puddles in low spots. Along both sidelines, the players stood in hooded slickers—the Aldridge High Panthers in red and the Coal Hill Miners in gold trimmed with green.

Despite the rain the grandstands were packed. On each side of the field, an unbroken ripple of umbrellas sloped upward from the front row and away to the top row. The Aldridge High fans were out in force. They had more than the spectacle of a girl catching passes to bring them out on this cold and rainy October evening. Their Panthers, for the first time in almost a dozen years, were playing for the championship.

On the field Denny Hoyt, the Panthers' place kicker, was kneeling down to fit the ball on the tee for the game's opening kickoff.

Frank, almost indistinguishable from the players in his hooded red slicker, watched Denny and wondered about the validity of his only football superstition. It was silly, of course, but Frank always had considered winning the coin toss to be a good omen. Tonight the Panthers had lost the toss—for the first time in this season of victories.

Frank shrugged off the thought. Football games were won by blocks and tackles, and by runs and passes, not by the luck of the call when the referee flipped a coin through the air.

The Miners—eleven of them taking up positions for the kickoff, the remainder standing at the sideline in their slickers—looked bigger than Frank had expected. He knew, of course, that the Miners were a big, tough, physical team with the strength to make their system work. But still their size surprised him. He reflected that Coach Warren Collins would not be the first football coach in history to trim a few pounds in the roster list he furnished for the printed programs.

The combination of the size of the Miners—big people, difficult to shove around—and the condition of the playing field—soggy and slippery, making for slow and uncertain going—concerned Frank.

Maybe the superstition about the coin toss wasn't so silly, after all.

Frank glanced down the row of his players lining the sideline for the kickoff. He found Jill, her hands thrust into the pockets of her slicker, standing between Richie Fields and Eddie McMahon. With the rest of them, she stared through the rain at the scene on the field, expressionless and silent in this moment before the beginning.

Jill had listened attentively when Frank, with Scott at his side, explained in a corner of the dressing room the difficulties, and the risks, of running patterns and catching passes in the rain.

She had nodded when Frank pointed out the obvious: Yes, the ball was going to be wet, a bit slippery, and, yes, the rain-soaked field meant unsure footing. She frowned slightly and glanced at Scott, then nodded her understanding when Frank explained that the passes were going to be a bit different tonight—less zip because the throwing hand was gripping a wet ball, and thrown with less of a lead because the receiver was sure to be a step slow on the wet grass.

She understood Frank's meaning but seemed hardly concerned when he explained the dangers posed by an opponent trying to defend against the pass on wet turf. A defensive halfback might skid into her or slam into her or fall on her, quite unintentionally, because of the slippery footing. She must be extra careful, he warned. In a threatening situation she must forget the pass and protect herself, he ordered.

"Okay, sure, yes," Jill said.

"I mean it," Frank said.

She frowned slightly and nodded. "I understand," she said seriously.

Denny kicked and followed through, sending the ball end over end up into the arc-lights glittering in the rain and down into the hands of the Coal Hill kick returner on the twelve-yard line.

The Panthers' tacklers thundered down the field toward him.

The Miners' blockers collected themselves in the center of the field, hoping to create a cocoon the runner could enter—and then explode out the other side.

But the runner never made it to the cocoon. He caught the ball cleanly, but a foot slipped when he tried to dart forward. He almost fell, then recovered himself, and began moving upfield. The lost step was costly, and Georgie and Henry hit him almost simultaneously on the twenty-one-yard line, dumping him to the ground.

The Miners sent their fullback, a low-slung heavyweight whose tree-trunk legs seemed never to stop pumping, into the line three straight times. He gained four yards, four yards, and three yards for a first down on the thirty-two-yard line.

Then the Panthers' defense, led by Georgie, stiffened and stopped the Miners, forcing a punt from the thirty-six-yard line.

Frank sent the offensive unit onto the field—with Lenny Parker at wide receiver—leaving Jill standing on the sideline. Lenny's blocking was worth more in the early going in the rain than Jill's pass-catching talents.

Throughout the first quarter, with the rain still drizzling down, the two teams battled between the thirty-yard lines, neither able to punch across the fifty-yard line under its own power.

The Miners' fullback worked overtime, hitting the line with almost monotonous regularity. Once he gained seven yards, bursting through inside tackle. But his other gains were two, three, four yards—always a little short of the yardage needed to sustain a drive to the end zone. Lacking a yard or two and facing fourth down, the Miners punted time and again.

Richie bore the brunt of the load for the Panthers' offense, slashing into the line. Marty bounced off tackles twice for good gains—six yards on one run and five on another. But the Panthers also were unable to keep a march going. Time and again they were short a needed yard or two and had to punt the ball away.

Frank sent Jill into the game for one series of downs. On the first play, Scott faked a pass to her to the right and then pitched out to Marty churning around left end. Frank watched Marty gather in the ball and tuck it away. Then he turned back to Jill.

Jill, running her pattern, was obviously learning a lesson that couldn't be taught on a basketball court—a basketball court of dry, varnished wood, not wet, slippery earth. It was a lesson that couldn't be learned on a dry football field, either, for that matter.

She ran in a heavy-footed way, certainly feeling the slipperiness of the field. And when she made her cut to the sideline, her feet slipped enough to put a startled expression on her face. Despite Frank's warning, the slippery footing had surprised her.

Twice more she ran her patterns without the ball going to her, and then she returned to the sideline while the Panthers punted the ball away once again.

Frank moved down the sideline toward Jill as the Miners put the ball in play on their twenty-eight-yard line.

"How'd it feel out there?"

Jill turned to him and said, "Oooooh."

"Yeah. Different." He paused, watching the play on the field. Then he said, "Can you make the play—I mean, catch a pass and get out of bounds?"

She nodded. "I think so. Yes."

"I don't want you stuck flat-footed inbounds with the ball in your hands."

She nodded again and said, "I can do it."

On the field the Miners were grinding out the yardage. The big fullback was going into the left side of the line, then the right side, then back to the left—gains of four, five, three yards—time and again.

Then, out of nowhere, the running back trailing the big fullback's powerful blocking burst through the line into an open spot in the secondary. He planted a foot on probably the only firm piece of earth on the field, executed a turn, and ran around one tackler, barely outstepped another, and raced to the fourteen-yard line before a Panther coming across bounced him out of bounds. The quarter ended, and the teams changed ends of the field.

Five plunges into the line later, the big fullback powered his way into the end zone, and the Miners kicked the extra point for a 7–0 lead.

Four minutes remained in the second quarter.

The Panthers had the ball on their own forty-six-yard line—their deepest penetration of the game.

The score remained at 7–0.

The rain, barely more than a mist now, seemed ready to quit.

On the field Jill lined up at wide receiver as Scott reached under the center and called out the signals.

Twice Scott had faked a pass to her before handing off into the line. This time he was going to throw to her if she succeeded in getting into the open at the sideline.

Frank watched the defensive halfback opposite Jill. Had the Panthers, with nothing but fakes to Jill and a steady diet of runs by Richie and Marty and Scott, lulled him into carelessness? It was too much to hope for. But maybe . . .

Scott took the snap. He stepped back, raised up, and pumped the ball once in Jill's direction. Then he brought the ball down and turned toward Richie, once again extending the ball to him.

The linebackers committed themselves, and Richie hit the line empty-handed as Scott withdrew the ball at the last moment.

Jill, working her way downfield carefully, turned toward the sideline in front of the backpedaling defensive back. Scott stepped back and turned, the ball on his hip, trying to trick the world into thinking his part of the play was done, with Richie powering into the center of the line.

The defensive back quit backpedaling and began moving with Jill toward the sideline. Then he moved forward to narrow the gap between them.

Frank clenched his fists. The defensive back was too close to Jill. Her brilliant faking maneuvers lost too much in the careful stepping required by the slippery surface of the playing field.

But the ball was on its way.

It was not a true Scott Butler bullet pass. Coming out of the fake throw and then the fake handoff, Scott may have hurried himself, may have taken less than a firm grip on the ball. Or maybe simply the wetness of the ball took its toll on his grip.

The ball wobbled slightly in its spiral. It floated—almost hung there—in the air. And it was off-target—just a bit—coming in a few crucial inches short of the necessary lead required to allow Jill a reception without breaking the forward motion carrying her out of bounds.

Jill, looking back, saw that she was outrunning the trajectory of the ball, and she slowed—but too late.

The defensive back was behind her, and with her, step for step.

Jill, concentrating on the ball, seemed oblivious to the hovering figure of the defensive back behind her.

Frank said aloud, barely above a whisper, "Let it go, let it go."

But Jill threw a hand up, a little behind her, shoulder high, and made a stab for the ball.

She got a part of it. Her outstretched hand was coming

up as the ball arrived. The ball caromed off her hand into the air.

The defensive back, behind her, reached up and picked the ball out of the air. He ran past Jill with nothing but space between him and the goal line.

Then Jill dived at his back.

CHAPTER

Jill slammed a shoulder into his backside at waist height, locking her arms around him.

He stumbled through one more step and then began to fall, turning sideways with the weight of Jill dragging on him.

They hit the ground side by side with Jill still hugging his waist.

Frank felt all the air go out of his lungs, as if he had received a kick in the chest. Then he felt a sudden feverish flushing in his face. He stood, for a moment that seemed like hours, without moving.

The scene that flashed before his eyes was like a series of still photographs flicking past, each offering up a bit more of horrible confirmation that the impossible was, indeed, possible. It was happening before his eyes.

Now, again for a moment that seemed like hours, the

two of them lay there—the defensive back hugging the ball, Jill next to him, one arm pinned under his body, the other arm clinging to his waist.

Scott appeared in the picture. Then Marty.

Frank, finally able to move after a moment—or hours—of stunned paralysis, took a couple of steps onto the field.

The referee, racing to the scene, waved Frank back.

Frank stopped but did not retreat back across the sideline.

Jill released the hold of her right arm, and the defensive back rolled off her left arm and got up.

Then Jill sprang to her feet.

Frank heard Scott shout, "Are you all right?"

Jill turned. The left side of her red uniform was brown with mud. Her cheek had mud on it.

She was grinning.

Frank stood in the center of the dressing room floor, all eyes on him, in the last minutes before taking the field for the start of the second half.

What was there to say?

The rain-swept field, combined with the overwhelming size of the Coal Hill Miners, was robbing the Panthers of the most effective weapons in their arsenal. Jill was slowed and uncertain in the course of running her patterns on the slippery surface. The Panthers' passing threat was severely reduced. Marty's skipping, dancing style of running around the ends lost a lot in the heavy footing. He was unable to deliver the sudden burst of speed—the instant acceleration—that always sent him zipping around corners, beyond the outstretched hands of tacklers. Richie was hitting the line, but his blockers were finding the oversized Miners hard to handle.

Frank glanced at Jill seated on a bench next to Henry. What was there to say to her?

Her tackle had saved a touchdown. She was enough of an athlete to make the tackle without hurting herself. So the horrible moment had turned out to be not horrible at all. Frank knew, now that it was over, that the play had held the possibility of a much worse horror—if Jill had caught the ball. The defensive halfback was there, ready to slam her to the ground before she took the first step toward the sideline. In retrospect, Scott's bad pass was a blessing.

So Frank had simply said to Jill, "Don't ever do that again—ever!"

"But he had a clear field in front of him," Jill said. "He would have scored a touchdown—with my pass."

Frank had to consciously restrain himself from grinning at her indignant protest. Jill Winston was a competitor, for sure. He said it again, "Don't ever do that again—ever!"

Jill nodded, and Frank frowned, knowing that her competitive instincts would send her flying toward the back of the ball carrier if the same thing happened again.

Frank turned slowly now, looking at the faces turned up at him. He took a deep breath and began speaking.

"They're big," he said, "and it's tough trying to move them." He paused. "So obviously what we need to do is go over them and around them, and that's tough to do in the rain."

Frank's statements hardly qualified as news bulletins with the mud-spattered players around him—linemen who were struggling at a weight disadvantage, runners who found neither openings nor sure footing, and a girl pass receiver deprived of the firm ground needed for her ballerina magic on the sideline.

"If we can't move them around and can't go over and around them, then we must make them move themselves." He stopped for a moment to let the statement sink in. The room was silent. "We can make them move themselves by being unpredictable. We'll sometimes pass when the situation calls for a run. We'll sometimes circle the ends when all the rules call for a plunge. Sometimes we'll have to pay a price for the strategy. If a pass fails where a plunge may have netted the couple of yards needed, we'll be paying for our strategy. But if you—you, the players on the field—make these plays work often enough, we'll knock the Miners off balance, leave them uncertain, make them tentative, perhaps lure them out of position."

Frank again turned slowly, looking at the serious faces peering up at him.

"A defense that is tentative, uncertain, a little off-balance, a bit out of position—that's a defense that can be penetrated, no matter how big and how strong, and no matter how slippery the playing field."

Frank nodded briefly, stepped to the door, opened it, and sent the players back out to the field.

The rain had stopped falling and most of the puddles had drained away, but the playing surface remained a soggy and slippery mass of mud beneath wet grass.

Frank put a change in place in the Panthers' offense even before the Miners kicked off to open the second half. He sent Richie back with Marty, putting them in tandem for the kickoff return.

The Miners took note of the change. The kicker placing the ball on the tee called out something to his bench across the field. The Coal Hill coach called out something in return. Then the kicker backed up and positioned himself, awaiting the referee's signal for the kickoff.

Frank nodded slightly with satisfaction at the indication that the Miners were not viewing the change as anything worthy of concern. Probably they were attributing the change to the wet field. Two kick returners reduced the chance of the receiver having to run to catch the ball, and perhaps even being forced to catch the ball on the run, risking a fumble at the worst and losing his footing at the best. If so, they were mistaken.

The referee swung his arm, and the kicker came forward and booted the ball, a high kick, sure to be shorter than hoped for.

Richie, on the right, moved over toward the center of the field, a half dozen steps forward, and took in the ball on the seventeen-yard line. He angled back to his right, heading toward the sideline and upfield, moving carefully on the slippery surface.

The Miners rushing downfield veered their charge toward the sideline, to intercept him.

Richie slowed, then stopped. He turned and threw the ball across the field, slightly behind him, in a long, lofting lateral to Marty.

Marty was alone. He waited for the lofting lateral like a punt returner, caught it, and turned and raced for the left sideline.

The Coal Hill tacklers were all going the wrong way.

Marty reached the sideline at the thirty-five-yard line and scampered untouched past the forty, the forty-five, the fifty.

The Miners, trying to recover, whirled and veered course and took off after him.

Marty zipped across the forty-five, the forty, the thirty-five.

On a dry field Marty would have been uncatchable.

And on this wet field he was uncatchable. He crossed the goal line untouched.

Denny kicked the extra point to tie the game, 7–7.

From there, through the third quarter and halfway into the fourth quarter, the two teams settled back into a grinding struggle between the thirty-yard lines—but with a difference.

Time and again the Panthers pulled the unexpected.

Lenny Parker, obviously replacing Jill because of his blocking ability, twice was the target of a Scott Butler pass. He caught one for eleven yards. The other whistled through his outstretched hands. The Miners had to keep an eye on Lenny.

When Jill was in the game, she ran her patterns, drawing a lot of attention—but receiving no passes. She was valuable as a decoy. But then the Miners started paying less attention to her, perhaps thinking that the Panthers were fearful of risking more bodily contact for her.

Twice Scott passed to Eddie McMahon when the short-yardage situation clearly called for a plunge into the line. Eddie, open because the Miners were geared for a plunge, caught one for a first down. Scott overthrew him on the other, forcing the Panthers to punt.

Neither team was able to break a long play for a touchdown, and neither team was able to sustain a drive to the end zone.

But Frank knew, as he stalked the sideline, that the Panthers were winning the war of attrition—a yard here, two yards there, gained in the exchange of the ball—slowly backing up the Miners.

The gambling plays designed to knock the Miners a little off balance, plant a seed of uncertainty, widen the range of possibilities the defense had to think about, force an occasional mistake—these were working often enough to do the job. The signs were there for Frank to see. A linebacker would hesitate a moment before slamming himself into the line to help stop a plunge. Charging linemen were wary as they moved in, and therefore slower.

Now, with six and a half minutes left on the clock, the

Panthers were taking over on the Miners' forty-one-yard line following Marty's twenty-two-yard punt return.

Jill jogged onto the field with the offense unit. Scott leaned into the huddle and said something, and the players lined up.

It took the Miners a moment to notice that something was different.

The Panthers had flipped the backfield. Jill was out wide—to the left, not the right. Richie, behind Scott, had Marty angled off to his right, not his left.

The Coal Hill defenders scurried and chattered and then, with a wave of the hand of a linebacker, the defensive captain, they settled into their positions.

A defensive halfback was out wide with Jill. But he was not the defensive halfback who had been shadowing Jill on every play and had grabbed off one of her passes. Jill's enduring shadow was across the field, and she was facing a defender who had not tracked her a single time.

Frank was a bit surprised that the Miners, for whatever reason, did not switch the defensive halfbacks to keep their strongest pass defender on Jill's side of the field. Perhaps the Miners, forced to make a quick judgment, decided there was not enough time. A quick snap from center could leave them in the midst of the shift and hopelessly vulnerable.

Scott took the snap, straightened up, and threw a quick pass to Jill going out of bounds. She grabbed the ball and stepped across the line, a five-yard gain to the thirty-six-yard line. She left the defensive halfback in a confused state of flat-footed embarrassment.

On the next play the Miners switched the defensive halfbacks, and Jill, in her new position to the left, found herself staring into the familiar face of her shadow. Scott sent Richie into the line for four yards. Then he sneaked two yards for a first down on the Miners' thirty-yard line.

Frank signaled Scott to flip the backfield back into its normal position. Everyone would be more comfortable, and particularly Jill, whose entire experience had been on the right side.

Scott gained four on a keeper to the right while Jill, out in front of him, went deeper than usual, pulling the defensive halfback with her and distracting a linebacker. Richie hit a solid wall of defense in the middle for no gain, and Marty picked up three yards behind Henry on the right side of the line.

The Panthers faced fourth down with three yards to go on the Miners' twenty-four-yard line.

Scott, approaching the huddle, glanced at Frank at the sideline. To Frank, there was no choice. The Panthers had never been so close and might never be so close again. Time was running out. He nodded to Scott and made a chopping motion with his right hand. This was no time to try a plunge against the mountainous Coal Hill line. This was no time to send Marty skipping around end on slippery turf. A quarterback sneak was an odds-on gamble with three yards needed against giant linemen. Throw the ball to Jill, the signal said.

When the Panthers lined up, the crowd on both sides

of the field rose to their feet with a roar. The Panthers were going for it on fourth down. They were not going to try a punt angled sharply toward the sideline, aimed at putting the Miners' backs to the wall. They were not going to ask Denny Hoyt to attempt the impossible—a field goal kick of more than forty yards. They were going to punch ahead, going for a touchdown.

Then suddenly the crowd went silent. The players alongside Frank at the sideline stood motionless, silent.

Frank had seen it many times: a close game between two good teams coming down to one play—a single play—that held victory in the balance. The team that won in that single play won the game.

This was such a play, Frank knew, and he was sure the Miners knew it, too.

Frank watched the opposing team's defense. A linebacker seemed a half step wider, as if poised to help defend against a sideline pass. The defensive halfback, teeth clenched, stared hard at Jill, as if certain beyond doubt that the play was coming at him. The Miners' linemen dug in for the charge after the passer.

Frank wondered with a sigh if there was anyone on the field or in the grandstands—or in the whole world—who did not know the play was going to be a pass to Jill Winston.

Frank looked at Jill. She was standing easily. Jill Winston had been in enough one-point basketball games to understand pressure.

Scott took the snap and backpedaled. Then he began moving to his right, trying to lure forward the defenders patrolling the area where Jill would be running a button-hook pattern at the sideline, seven yards downfield.

The defenders did not take the lure, particularly the linebacker. He moved a step farther toward Jill's route. Jill loped straight ahead, headed for a spot between the linebacker and the defensive back. The defensive back was backpedaling furiously to keep himself between the goal and the advancing Jill.

Scott stopped his movement to the right, all pretense of a run gone.

Jill dipped a shoulder, turned to her left, and stopped the advancing linebacker in his tracks. Then she whirled back. Her feet slipped, but she maintained her balance and headed for the sideline.

The defensive back was with her every step of the way.

The linebacker, recovering, started moving toward her again.

Scott pumped once but held the ball. The defensive back had Jill bottled up. He was sticking with her on every movement. They were like two dancers who had rehearsed the act. Jill could not shake him. And the linebacker kept edging toward them.

Scott quickly glanced across the field, looking for Marty in the left flat and Eddie McMahon drifting into the secondary on the left. Nothing there. A tackler rushing across with his eye on Scott was too close to Marty. A defensive back had picked up Eddie and had him covered.

Scott looked back to his right, no longer seeking Jill

but desperately looking for any kind of an opening, and started tucking the ball away for a run.

Tacklers were fighting their way through.

Then there was a shout—"Scott!"

Jill, breaking away from the sideline, was running across the field, parallel to the line of scrimmage, toward the center of the field, about ten yards downfield.

She had left behind the defensive back, who now was sprinting at full speed after her.

The linebacker, caught going the wrong way when Jill accelerated, started to turn and chase the form flashing past him. But then he spotted Scott tucking the ball away and moved forward to block a run.

Scott brought up the ball and cocked his arm, at precisely the moment that Frank shouted from the sideline, "*No!*"

But the ball was on the way.

Jill, plunging forward, got her outstretched right hand on the ball as she crossed the hash mark at the fourteen-yard line. A fraction of a second later she clapped her left hand on the ball. Then she pulled the ball in and tucked it away.

For a moment she seemed to lose her balance and almost fell in her headlong forward plunge. Then she righted herself and veered to her right, toward the goal.

The defensive back—her shadow—was closing in. The other defensive back abandoned Eddie and joined the chase.

Jill outran them to the goal and raced into the end zone untouched.

Frank left the madhouse of the dressing room and stepped out into the madhouse of the corridor, heading for his office to bring Jill back to the dressing room.

The shouting in the crowded corridor was deafening.

Frank, smiling, held both hands above his head to acknowledge the cheers, and the noise got even louder.

He began inching his way through the crowd, taking the slaps on the back, nodding his thanks for the congratulations from the elated fans, and finally reached the door to his office. He knocked, and Jill opened the door a crack.

"Let's go," he said.

CHAPTER

18

On Monday morning Frank was not surprised when Jill appeared in his office door a few minutes after the bell sounded ending the second period. He was seated at his desk performing his Monday morning ritual of reviewing the schedule for the practice week and the game plan he and Ron had drawn up over the weekend for the Prescott High Badgers.

Prescott High was a smaller school and a nonconference opponent for the Panthers. They stacked up as the perfect team to play following the grueling Coal Hill game clinching the championship. The Badgers seemed to pose no serious problems for the Panthers. But Frank remembered that Johnson City was a smaller school and a nonconference opponent, the perfect opponent for a season opener, seeming to pose no serious problems for the Panthers.

In some ways the scare delivered by the Johnson City Trojans seemed years, not just six weeks, ago. But in other ways the horror of the narrow escape remained vivid in Frank's mind, a lesson not to be forgotten. So he was giving the Prescott High Badgers every bit of the attention to detail that he had given the Coal Hill Miners, the Hutchinson Wildcats, and every other North-Central Conference foe.

Frank had neither seen nor talked to Jill over the weekend. The time had long since passed when he felt a need to call her—to gain reassurance that her father had not changed his mind, to measure her reaction to nuisance callers, to guide her in handling sportswriters' calls. The various calls had fallen off to nothing, and the questions in Frank's mind had vanished. He had spent most of Saturday and Sunday working in the training room—viewing and then re-viewing the game tape—and nothing had brought Jill to the school. So they had not met over the weekend.

Frank's last sight of her had been her exit from the dressing room, with her father briefly visible through the open door as she left. To Frank's surprise, Palmer Winston had not accosted him with angry words about the two dangerous lapses in their agreement: Jill making a tackle and Jill taking a pass in the center of the field, vulnerable to a tackle.

At the time Frank had wondered why.

"Come in, Jill," Frank said, getting to his feet and walking around the desk. "Have a chair." He walked past her and closed the office door, then returned to his seat behind the desk. He smiled at her as she sat down across from him. "Cutting your third-period study hall again, I see," he said.

Jill smiled back at him in remembrance of the two third-period interviews eight weeks earlier. "Coach, I—"

"What is it, Jill?"

She took a deep breath. "Coach, I'm going to quit the football team and go back to basketball." She paused and then added in a voice barely above a whisper, "Sign-up is today."

Frank watched her. Then he said, "All right."

Jill looked surprised. "All right?"

Frank smiled. "Of course, all right. It's your decision to make. Same as coming out for football in the first place."

Jill looked past Frank, a somber expression on her face. "I feel awful," she said.

"There's nothing for you to feel awful about."

"Well, I feel like I'm letting everybody down. There are three games left. Everybody is counting on me. But basketball—"

Frank cut her off with a laugh. "We've won the championship—and on your touchdown."

She looked at Frank a moment. "You think it'll be all right, then?"

"Yes, I do." Then he asked, "When did you make this decision?"

"I don't know, really. Last week, some time, I guess."

"You mean, before the Coal Hill game."

She nodded. "Yes, before the game."

Yes, Frank thought, before the Coal Hill game. That was why she made a diving tackle to save a touchdown. That was why she broke to the center of the field for a pass. She was guaranteeing that the championship was won before she departed. There was going to be no next game for her. This was the last chance. And there was no risk of an angry Palmer Winston withdrawing permission for her to play. She was through playing football anyway.

"Do your parents know of your decision yet?"

She nodded again. "Yes."

"They knew before the game?" Frank asked.

"I told them on the way to the stadium on Friday night."

Yes, Frank thought, her parents knew going into the game. And after the game Palmer Winston filed no protest with him at the dressing room door because he already knew there would be no more flying tackles, no more runs with the ball through a broken field of tacklers. He knew it was over.

"I see" was all that Frank said.

Jill wrinkled her forehead into a frown. "You don't seem surprised," she said.

"I don't think I am, really," Frank said. "Everything seems very right this way."

She nodded, gave a little smile, and stood up.

Frank got to his feet.

"What about Prescott, and Burlington, and the Fayette Pioneers?" she asked.

Frank smiled at her. "We'd win a lot easier with you in there catching passes, that's for sure," he said. "But I'm betting that we'll win anyway. The Panthers have developed a taste for winning, a winning habit."

She started toward the door, then turned back, seeming to hesitate.

"Yes?" Frank prompted.

She tilted her head slightly. "Nobody else knows," she said. "Just you, my parents, me—not even Henry."

Frank lifted an eyebrow. And not even Elaine Carter, he thought. The Aldridge High girls' basketball coach was heading for a very large and very pleasant surprise.

"What I mean is," Jill said, "could I tell the team? You know, sort of explain, so maybe they'd understand why—"

"Sure, of course," Frank said. "Before we go out for practice, okay?"

She smiled. "Thanks," she said.

When the first of the players, wearing pads and practice uniforms, started to head out of the dressing room for the field, Frank called out, "Hold it up just a minute. Stay in here until I come back."

He walked down the corridor to his office, got Jill, and returned with her to the dressing room. When Jill stepped into the dressing room—wearing jeans and a shirt instead of a football practice uniform—the room fell silent.

"Jill has something to say," Frank announced.

Jill looked around the dressing room for a moment and

then said, "I'm leaving the football team, and I'm going out for basketball." She paused a moment. "They need me, so that's where I belong now."

The silence still hung over the room.

Jill shrugged and grinned. "Well, that's about it, except that it's been fun, and we won the championship, and that was great, and"—the smile seemed to fade—"and you're a real sweet bunch of guys."

The silence this time lasted only about one second. "That's us—sweet," piped the burly Georgie Francis.

Georgie grinned into the laughter that followed his remark.

Jill smiled at the laughter around the room and said, "Now you'll probably go on to beat Prescott and Burlington and Fayette, just to show that you never needed me anyway."

The silence returned.

Jill turned to Frank. "I've got to"—she hesitated, as if not trusting her voice to speak the remaining words—"to go now." She nodded her head slightly in a sort of farewell salute, then turned and walked to the door and opened it.

Behind her, somewhere, the applause started and spread through the room.

Jill stopped in the door and turned.

Frank thought for a moment she was going to cry. Then he knew she wasn't.

Jill, tight-lipped, gave a little wave and disappeared out the door.